ACADEMY
FOR THE
GIFTED

GRANT
ACADEMY

est. 1894

HUDSON WARM

ACADEMY FOR THE GIFTED

ACADEMY FOR THE GIFTED

Cover Design: Lance Buckley (lancebuckley.com)
Editing: Melissa McCoubrey (melissamccoubrey.ca)
Formatting and Proofreading: Enchanted Ink Publishing

ISBN: 978-1-7354098-1-8
LCCN: 2021918544

Playlist

"And We Walk After" - Trevor Kowalski

"I Wanna Be Yours" - Arctic Monkeys

"Le Papillon Solitaire" - Franz Gordon

"Young and Beautiful" - Lana Del Rey

"You" - Petit Biscuit

"Choke" - IDKHBTFM

"Waltz of the Flowers" - Tchaikovsky

"Silhouettes of You" - Isaac Gracie

"Für Elise" - Ludwig van Beethoven

"Mystery of Love" - Sufjan Stevens

"Campus" - Vampire Weekend

"The Glass Slipper" - Martin Klem

"La Vie en Rose" - Edith Piaf

"La fille sans larmes" - Lo Mimieux

"Movement" - Hozier

"Once Upon a December (instrumental)" - Emile Pandolfi

"Locket" - Crumb

"Aphrodite" - Honey Gentry

Swan Lake Suite, op. 20: Scène - Tchaikovsky

"November" - Max Richter

THE KILLING

August 30, 10:47 p.m.

I DIDN'T WAKE up one day and choose to be a murderer. The thought had lingered for a while, never at the forefront. It was a balloon. I bounced it around, nurtured it, tried to dismiss it, unwittingly inflating it. I tried to bat it away. Tried to lose it in the clouds, have it tangle in some distant branch. But when I fed it too much air, it popped. The sound echoed in the chambers of my head, reminding me what I had to do. There was no other choice. So here I am.

It is almost too perfect, the way she lies on her stomach atop Asher McCoy's navy comforter in the dimly lit shadows, brown hair cascading down her back. Music posters, curled up in the corners, fill the blue walls. She doesn't suspect a thing as she faces the window.

She alternates between scrolling and texting.

I alternate between apprehension and determination.

This has gone on too long.

They would have wanted this for me.

My gloved fingers tremble on the hilt of my knife.

I think, for a moment, that it would be better to flip the blade toward myself.

Someone showers in the bathroom across from us. It is only a matter of time before I'll be caught, and standing here like a coward is not helping.

Why haven't I done it already?

Camilla is alone. Now is the perfect time.

Still, I am unsure if I'll be able to live as a murderer.

Making the choice for me, Camilla switches to the front-facing camera on her phone, half smiling for a self-ie before she sees me standing in the background on her screen, eyeing her with a knife in hand. Before she can scream, before she can process it, I lunge to cover her mouth with a pillow. Thankfully, the shower mutes her muffled cries.

Shh.

I can't look at her while I do it. So I close my eyes.

I close my eyes and turn her over.

I close my eyes and turn her over and jab the knife into her chest.

Blood saturates my gloves and the knife.

I have never done anything like this before.

I stumble backward toward the door, leaving it ajar.

Descend the stairs.

Beecher House will never be the same to me.

My hand shakes as I twist the doorknob, now bloody, and race across the empty campus. Everyone is at the par-ty; nobody sees me.

Salty tears sit on my cheeks.

I can't look at this bloody knife, nor can I leave it on the ground.

I want to stab myself, mix my blood with hers, but they wouldn't want that for me.

I did it for a reason, and if I die, it would be futile.

Rest in peace, Camilla Harding.

ƁEXLEY

Six Months Earlier

*Some are born great, some achieve greatness, and some
have greatness thrust upon 'em.*
—Shakespeare, *Twelfth Night*

ALL I'D EVER wanted was to become an eagle.

A Gifted Golden Eagle, that is.

Refresh.

We hovered around the wooden kitchen counter, my laptop next to a marble bowl of fake pears. The afternoon sunlight fell hot on my back, and the rustling of trees came in through the cracked-open door.

Refresh.

Dad peered over my shoulder, his breath humid on my neck.

Refresh.

"It's here!" I shouted, despite how close Mom, Dad, and Drew stood next to me.

Admissions update.

The alert flashed back at me, my mouse damp in my sweaty hand. I could find out right now if I simply pressed down. My stomach grumbled, partly because I was hungry but mostly because I was scared—scared that all my work had been pointless.

"Come on, Bex," Mom said. "You've been staring down the screen for thirty seconds."

I gulped and nodded. The hair on my forearms bristling, I clicked. It was time.

Dear Miss Bexley Windsor,

Congratulations! On behalf of the Grant Academy for the Gifted (GAFTG) community, I am pleased to offer you admission.

We are thrilled to welcome you aboard the flock of Gifted Golden Eagles. Through academic rigor and a vibrant social experience, we aim to shape you into a strong and sharp young leader and prepare you for success at elite universities. For over two hundred years, Upper School GAFTG students have graduated with extraordinary skills in and out of the classroom.

We have struggled to select the best eagles out of an abundance of highly qualified individuals. Your transcript, extracurricular activities, and essays stood out among thousands of applications. Here at the Academy, our principle values are respect, perseverance, and hard work. Joining our flock as a senior, your success will take a great deal of effort and endurance, but your application and talent have convinced us you are well-equipped for the challenge.

We expect your response by May 5 so we can prepare the Upper School for your admission by assigning you a residence and a class schedule. Please reach out to admissions@grantacademyforthegifted.com with any inquiries.

We look forward to having you!

Sincerely,
The Admissions Board

Dad erupted from his seat. Fireworks lit up the screen. The second I saw *Congratulations*, my wound-up nerves finally released. Mom shot up from her chair and proceeded to do an embarrassing happy dance. I cringed at her flailing arms but smiled within. This was the seed that would make my elaborate dreams for the future closer to becoming reality.

I played the film on the Grant Academy website for the seventh time today, imagining myself relaxing on the picturesque campus, a tree shadowing me. It looked perfect, almost too good to be true.

When my parents had told me I could finally apply this year, I'd thought they were joking. To be honest, the decision was likely out of fear and sympathy, though I had no complaints; I could finally get away from all this.

Away from Abigail's unfinished story.

Farewell, New Jersey. This was my ticket out of Vista High. I'd grasp it tightly, hold it close, and never let it go.

I

Parting is such sweet sorrow
That I shall say good night till it be morrow.
—Shakespeare, *Romeo and Juliet*

THE VIEW OUT the car window was a stock photograph of tenuous clouds and gentle waves. Warm-colored trees scattered the mountains, and my ears plugged as we ascended due to the increasing altitude.

Two hours to go, but I wasn't complaining. I'd hardly survived a few weeks at summer camp, much less a year on some isolated New Hampshire mountain. The anticipation made me want to explode.

I removed an earbud. "How many minutes?"

"One minute less than when you asked a minute ago." Mom's clenched teeth nearly bit me through the rearview mirror. Her balayaged hair was tied in a loose bun, and her fair-skinned face was focused on the road.

"Someone remind me again why I'm here?" Drew ruffled his straggly blond hair. For the last four hours, his elbow had kept alternating off and on the armrest in a futile attempt to rest.

"So you can bid your older sister farewell," Mom said.

"You're gonna miss me, Drew. Just you wait."

He flipped me off, sneered, and returned to his attempted slumber.

It turned out two hours could pass rather quickly when spent rewatching favorite episodes of medical dramas on my phone. Before I knew it, Dad nudged me from the passenger seat, and Drew ripped out my left earbud.

Grant Academy for the Gifted.

The platinum letters decorated skinny pillars of an intimidating wrought iron gate that stretched across the road's horizontal entirety and into the grass. On the tops of two columns sat the school mascot: Gifted Golden Eagles, painted in gold with white heads. Through the bars, a sprawling building stretched before me, gargoyles looking tiny in the distance.

"Kinda like prison bars," Drew said, gesturing to the gate and cracking a smile.

"Great observation," I said sarcastically as a knot formed in the pit of my stomach.

This place seemed so . . . official. Mom had said the Academy was like a college campus, but when we visited those last year, they seemed more lighthearted: kitschy souvenir shops, students traipsing around in pajamas. Here, no students were visible, yet I could tell they wouldn't be wearing sweats.

Everything I'd worked so hard for. Everything I'd dreamed of. It was here. But now a part of me wished to turn back. The vibe this place emitted was wintry and cold, and it was still August.

"Time?" I never wore a watch, but Drew couldn't be found without his ugly square one.

"Nine fifty-eight," he grunted.

Dad crossed his arms. "Assuming we're the only ones who get here before the gates even open?"

"I'm sensing passive aggression from you." Mom emphasized *I'm*, probably something their couples' therapist told her to do. "The least we can do is act civil to see her off."

Ever since Mom had taken up yoga two years ago, she'd been all about zen and peace and all that. Now she was an instructor and a hardcore yogi. She'd tried to get Dad on board, but he preferred a strict daily regimen of the same workouts. He was like that with his work as an author, too. He'd lock himself in a room for exactly three and a half hours every day. Mom, Drew, and I always knew better than to knock.

"I'm acting plenty civil! I just don't see why we had to wake up at—"

A sudden sharp ringing tone commenced the opening of the gate, forcing a yelp out of Dad. A chill descended my spine as the gate made way for us to pass. The hill was steep and windy, groomed foliage of green, purple, and orange decorating the borders.

Hiccups came from the driver's seat. Oh, no.

I began, "Are you—"

Dad patted her shoulder. "Let out the waterworks, honey." Her melodrama would be one thing I wouldn't miss.

Our tires gritted up the asphalt. We pulled in, the one Honda in a parking lot of Range Rovers. The collar of my white polo shirt stuck out the top of my evergreen

GAFTG sweatshirt with embroidered gold lettering, a plaid pleated skirt beneath it. This outfit—something I wouldn't usually wear—was the one part of me that fit in here.

Dad popped the trunk so we could gather my bags, and I nearly collapsed from the weight of all my over-packing: two duffels and two suitcases.

"Here, I got it," Dad said. He took a duffel, as did a reluctant Drew. Mom and I both took a suitcase.

Painted white arrows on the blue rock trail led us up a never-ending hill. I'd never seen such stunning foliage, such tall evergreens. Eventually, people started to fill my vision. Faculty, students—hurried bodies that never seemed to slow down. Chatter flooded my ears.

"Wow." Even Drew was impressed, which was saying something.

Parents were only allowed this far, so I kissed Mom, Dad, and Drew on the cheeks, receiving an "ew" from Drew.

"See ya, Bex." Dad's calm facade seemed close to breaking.

Mom took my hand in hers. "You're gonna thrive here, Bex," she said, her voice cracking.

"I'll miss you. Expect a lot of calls, okay? I'll keep you updated on everything."

"You better." We spent a few minutes in a final hug—the last time in a while I'd be able to feel her safety and warmth.

Everything will be fine. Great, even.

Dad and Drew plopped the duffels on the ground, and Mom handed me the other suitcase. We said our final goodbyes, and as they walked off, I glanced at them and locked eyes with Drew. He was looking over his shoulder and seemed to be holding back tears. Maybe he would miss me after all. I'd be back for Thanksgiving break. That wouldn't be too long. I shot back a bittersweet smile. Eventually, they turned into tiny silhouettes and then disappeared down the hill.

When I turned to see the central campus, I blinked. This had to be some sort of dream. I'd seen the photos on the website, but in person, Grant Academy was unreal. One side building was grander than the whole of Vista High. Spires reached into the sky, and pointed arches of cobblestone stood in front. A gray gargoyle seemed to be staring right at me, its gaze piercing. Two turrets flanked the largest building, decorated in overgrown greenery. More stunning buildings filled my peripheral vision, built of stone and wood.

"Here for check-in?" A bearded man with glasses approached me. "Name?"

"Oh, um, Bexley Windsor."

He flipped through pages on a clipboard. "There you are. New student from New Jersey. Congratulations! Welcome to Grant Academy for the Gifted. We're glad to have you. One of our volunteers will lead you to your dorm. You'll be in room 315A with"—he glanced down at the page once more—"Venus Herrington. Oh, she's a funny one, that girl. In my history course last year."

I managed a stilted smile, kicking the blue rock to calm my nerves. Venus had reached out to me in May, but besides sporadic texts and a single video call, we were pretty much strangers.

"Bates!" He summoned a man from a circle of gossiping teachers. "Lead Miss Windsor to her dorm, room 315A, will you?"

"Gladly. Here, follow me. And let me help you with those," he said, referencing my bags. The formidable man had a left side part of brunette hair and green eyes. He wore a navy sweater-vest over his pink long sleeve. "Mr. Bates, calculus professor." With disconcerting formality, he shook my hand, his fierce grip a startle. He smelled leathery as a fresh new car. "That's how we do handshakes here. Firm. Professional." He spoke with a faint but recognizable British lilt.

Another awkward smile. Something about this man was strange. I felt his eyes on me as I gazed at the dreamy Tudor cottages on the blue rock trail beside us.

"The teacher boardinghouses," he said, as if reading my mind. The wheels of my suitcase rolled behind him.

Ivy climbed up the huge buildings surrounding us, designed with medieval architecture and beautiful windows. "How do people not get lost around here?"

He held the door as we entered one of the Gothic buildings and led me through a narrow marble corridor. The sound of his dress shoes hitting the floor echoed around us.

"Well, perhaps a friend could give you a look around. I would if I didn't have to get back to the commons. I volunteered to be a greeter to get out of a meeting." He bent down to meet my level and placed an index finger on his lips, as if letting me in on a secret. "But if I'm being completely honest, I still get lost. And it's my fifth year here."

"Wow." I said the first word that sprang to mind, not sure exactly what was wowing me. Everything, really.

The interior was filled with a stunning array of paintings. Perhaps one day one of mine could hang here; art had always been a passion of mine. Compared to some other kids my age, I wasn't very skilled, but for me, art was an outlet.

"You'll be just fine. Lucky for you, 315A is easy. First building by the entrance, third floor. Just gotta ascend these stairs and find number 315."

A wooden door opened to a spiral staircase with metallic railings. "This is amazing."

"You'll get used to it," he said in a reassuring tone.

I followed his shadow up the long sturdy staircase, still in utter awe of my surroundings. By the end, I was fatigued, sweaty, and ready to finally see my room.

"I'm not allowed in the girls' dorms, so this is where I leave you." The word *allowed* came off his tongue oddly.

"Okay. Thanks, Mr. Bates."

"Any time. Perhaps you'll even be in my class!"

"Yep!"

He passed me the suitcase he'd dragged and lingered there for a moment too long, as if he were preparing to say something. Darting around the corner, I got rid of him to find number fifteen. Without a doubt, fifteen—my new home—was there, awaiting my entrance. I didn't have a key yet, but hopefully Venus would provide me one. Queen music echoed through the wall—Drew's favorite.

I gave three precise knocks, remaining silent in fear that my squeaky voice would betray me.

The music faded. "Yeah? Is that Bexley?"

I nodded, then said, "Yeah," after realizing she couldn't see my head movements through the door.

The knob screeched open, Venus behind it. "Bexley!" She pulled me into an awkward embrace.

I dropped the heavy weights from my arms, the crash reverberating as they hit the floor. The room held two beds, closets and desks on either side, and an embroidered lavender couch between the beds by the blinds-covered window. Above the couch hung an askew marble print.

"Glad you found your way okay." Venus wore a neon pink sweatshirt that contrasted nicely with her dark complexion. Her hair cascaded in thick black ringlets down her back and shoulders. She looked even prettier than she did in the social media profile I'd studied.

"Yeah, Mr. Bates showed me."

"Mr. Bates? Oof."

"What about him?"

"He's um . . . Well, you'll see." She plopped back down on her bed. This wasn't quite like roommate encounters from the movies. "How have you been liking the Academy so far?"

"I mean, I've been here for less than twenty minutes. But it's pretty, that's for sure."

"Yeah, they make it look all nice to distract the students from the dangers lurking within." She chuckled. "Just kidding."

Dangers?

"Oh." I laughed along. We maintained silent eye contact for a moment. "So, is there a lot of homework?" I asked, not sure what to say. Gazing around the room, my eyes caught on a heap of hangers, papers, and clothes. I swallowed down the neat freak within me.

"What? You're not one of those people who demands everything be folded, right?" Venus asked, lying on her stomach atop her black and rose-gold comforter. "Because if so, we will not be getting along."

"Pardon?"

"Sorry. You just seem like the type of person to see the world in checkboxes."

"Well, a few scattered sweaters won't bother me. And what's wrong with checkboxes?"

"Nothing." She laughed and reverted her attention to her phone, snapping selfies with flash. At once, Venus tossed her device on the carpeted floor beside her. "By the way, there's your schedule." She pointed to a piece of paper on the nightstand beside her bed. "Let's compare."

She snatched the printout before I could take a single look. "Euro history, calculus, physics—boring," Venus said.

As she continued to look over my schedule, I stared up at the beige stucco ceiling. Meeting new people was inevitably awkward, at least for me.

"They were required to graduate," I said flatly.

"That sucks. At the Academy, most seniors use their last year to take some fun classes." Her eyes skimmed the sheet. "Looks like we don't share any periods. My electives are all fashion-design related."

"Aw."

"How enthusiastic," she said. "Oh, by the way, I bought some posters for our room. I was thinking we could each choose two or three to hang up over our beds. They're vintage." She unrolled six posters of black-and-white magazine covers. "I don't know. I was thinking this girl in front of the Eiffel Tower kind of matched your aesthetic. If you don't like them, we can—"

"I *love* them," I interrupted, admiring the images. One

illustrated a woman wearing a large hat that veiled half of her face. Another looked like something straight from the twenties, with a woman on a couch, her skirt draping over the cushions, her hair chopped into a bob. Venus presented another one of an elegant woman in a kimono, holding a fan. "These are amazing."

"I'm so glad." Venus yawned. "I think I'm going back to bed. If you're awake, could you let me know when my room service comes?"

"There's room service? How fancy *is* this place?" I asked incredulously.

"If you couldn't already tell, they don't mind shedding a few pennies for the 'Next Generation of Leaders,'" she said with air quotes.

I snickered, this time a genuine response. *Next generation of leaders*—quite an expectation.

"Do you want help unpacking or setting your stuff up?" Venus offered.

"Uh, I mean—"

"Okay, good. I hate unpacking. Good night or . . . morning," she said, stifling another yawn.

"That would be great," I finished, whispering under my breath. Attending Grant had been my dream for so long. Last year, I'd ticked off a countdown daily on the dry-erase board in my room, awaiting the day I could finally start anew. Awaiting *today*. Why, then, did I feel nauseated?

Venus's lamp flickered off, making the room difficult to navigate. I'd have to wait to unpack. For now, I could nap. If only I had my bed set up. *Ugh.*

II

Death lies on her like an untimely frost
Upon the sweetest flower of all the field.
—Shakespeare, *Romeo and Juliet*

I FOLDED A pair of tan trousers on a clothing hanger. Dusk streamed through the window, casting the room in a golden glow. Though I was glad we didn't have to wear uniforms, I didn't have many outfits that fit within the strict dress code. After last autumn at the lake house, I'd thrown out pretty much my whole suitcase. Everything had reminded me of her. Mom and I went on a huge shopping spree over the summer to replenish my wardrobe.

I wanted to stay in the dorm the night of August 30.

But I'd only known Venus for a day. We were at that stage in which I'd blindly agree to anything; I needed to make a good impression.

"Don't you wanna meet everyone?" she said, legs crossed on the lavender couch.

No, not really. "I mean . . ."

"It'll be so much fun," she coaxed. "And I won't leave your side." Venus blinked at me with puppy dog eyes.

"I need to organize my stuff." I gestured to the pile of clothes atop my bare mattress. "And I still want to finish setting up everything on my bed." Last night I had slept with a mere blanket.

"Listen, I'll help you with all of that tomorrow, okay?" She took a furry blanket from her bed and tossed it on mine. "That's all you'll need to sleep. It's super comfortable. I promise."

I sighed, stroking the fur. "It is pretty soft."

"Tonight will be so much fun."

"Eh, I'm not sure. I can't sleep on my mattress with all that clothing covering it."

Venus rolled her eyes, then swung her arm at the clothes, knocking them all on the ground. "Problem solved."

"Hey! Those were folded!" I protested.

"The night's not getting any younger." Venus held up her watch.

"You're not gonna take no for an answer, are you?"

"Come on, *please*." Her smile told me she was used to getting her way.

We were almost out the door when Venus—dressed in a silky black dress with a plunging neckline—demanded I change. Her hair was tied up, lone pieces framing her face. Statuesque beauty radiated off her.

"It's only jeans," I said. "I always wear these."

"With zero holes? No way."

"Well, if you'd let me finish folding my clothes, I'd be able to pick—" I started.

Her eyes lit up as she raced to the dresser beside her bed. "Your green eyes will pop in this."

My eyes were blue.

The skinny strap of a tank top whipped me in the face as she threw it over her shoulder. "You can keep on your jeans, but at least put the tank on."

And so I did. Standing out was the last thing I wanted to do, and if Venus was trying to help me, I would take it. She smothered me in floral perfume before shutting the door behind us. Together, we strutted through the narrow corridor, impressive student artwork on the walls. Attempting to mirror her confident walk, I most likely resembled a penguin.

"Ooh, you're gonna meet everyone! This is so exciting."

I let out an awkward chuckle. "Yeah, I guess."

"Look at me." Venus eyed me up and down. "You're pretty, but you have to own yourself more."

"*Own* myself?"

"Exactly."

"Okay, just—where exactly are we headed?"

"Beecher House, one of the boys' residences. I kind of forget how to get there. We'll let the music guide us." She did some kind of wavy arm movement.

I laughed. "Aren't girls not supposed to go over there?"

Venus shrugged. "Everyone does it. And if you think about it, they can't expel the entire female student body."

Faces everywhere. Sweaty armpits. Strobe lights. Pounding music. I couldn't see much of the decor or furnishings in the darkness.

Venus took my hands and started dancing, swaying her hips to the beat. "Want a drink?" We jostled through the crowd as she took me over to the makeshift bar, much too big for some high school living situation, and poured me some who-knows-what. Red cups were scattered across the counter, some crumpled or ripped.

"No thanks." After last autumn, I swore I'd never drink again.

She laughed. "I'll take it, then. Wouldn't want to waste." She chugged it and slammed the red cup on the countertop. The room reeked of body odor and alcohol. "Seriously, it's so good. A sip won't kill you."

She shoved another cup in my face, its sharp liquor scent assaulting my nostrils. Purely to prevent causing a scene, I took it in my hands, put the rim to my lips, and pretended to down the drink, pouring the liquor out behind me. I hardly felt bad about staining the fuzzy carpet; the floor was already dirtied with pretzels, somehow sand, and—my goodness—was that cat hair? It was difficult to tell with the flashing lights.

"Hey, Venus!" shouted some guy behind her.

She ran to embrace him. "Suzuki! How've you been?"

"I'm all right. Fresh off the fourteen-hour plane ride from Osaka. Who's this?" He nodded his head toward me, and immediately I felt myself blush.

"Why don't you introduce yourself? Or actually, I can be your wingwoman. Her name's Bexley, and she's new." Her words were already slurred.

"Hi." My voice was squeaky.

"Hey. Chase. Most call me Suzuki, my last name." He was tall and lean, with lustrous raven hair that reached his ears. He wore a fancy-looking watch with a cracked face and held a black vape pen.

"It's a pleasure to meet you," I replied.

"Why so formal?" He chuckled. "You got your schedule yet?"

I nodded, pulling up a photo of it on my phone. "Do you have yours?"

My goodness, I suck at small talk.

He snatched my phone and scanned the little boxes. "Doesn't seem like we have anything together. Maybe some frees."

"Hopefully."

Hopefully? Did I really just say that?

Heat rose to my cheeks.

He cracked a proud grin, outstretching the hand with the vape. "Want?"

"I'm okay."

He shrugged, taking a long hit and exhaling a cloud of smoke to his left. "Hey, to each their own. See ya. Yo, boys!" Chase reverted his attention to a crowd, and soon he was off.

"Good choice. Suzuki never listens to me when I tell him it kills his lungs," Venus said. "Let me give you a little rundown." She neared my ear and began to whisper. "That was Chase. He's cocksure, can be funny, kind of an asshole at times. Next to him"—she pointed—"is Asher McCoy. This girl Jessie has been in love with him for, like, forever, but he friend zones her so hard. It's kind of funny, only because she's . . . not the sweetest. My advice: stay away from her. Then there's Eric, that blond one laughing right there. Petulant, but they tolerate him because his parents are, like, famous. Takes himself a little too seriously." The boy she gestured toward had a mop of light hair that covered his right eye. He wore a gray tee with a faded logo.

I nodded, trying to take it all in, overwhelmed.

She continued. "Then there's—"

"Venus!" It was Chase again. "Yo, we're playing truth or dare. Bring the newbie."

"Do you want to go?" she whispered.

"I mean—"

"Good. Come on."

I followed her shadow to a white couch in a corner of the room with all kinds of stains on it. People crowded around, some seated on the floor. "Ready to be traumatized?" Suzuki said.

Traumatized?

"Yo, look, it's everyone's favorite duo."

I turned to my right to find Venus rolling her eyes. Striding through the doorway were two girls, intimidating just from their postures. I cringed, watching everyone around them part to form a neat path for their entry.

"Camilla, Jessie, come play truth or dare!" shouted Eric.

"We just got here." The girl's voice was irritating simply from those four words. "But yeah, sure."

"That's Jessie," Venus whispered, rolling her eyes at the redhead waltzing in. Her hair fell to one side, cheekbones emphasized through her taut pale skin.

She rushed over to Asher's side and squished into the nonexistent space between him and Eric. "Who's she?" Jessie said, speaking as if I weren't there and gesturing toward me.

"*She's* Bexley," Chase said. Such a simple answer, though it made my cheeks blush.

"Hi, Bexley," Eric said, outstretching his arm, his voice throaty and raw. He had a slightly upturned nose and seemed to be the only boy whose words weren't garbled. "Eric Fernsby. Nice to meet you."

"You, too."

Some others joined us, squished on the couch. There were too many faces to keep track of; everyone looked the same to me, even if they shared no common features. I couldn't wait to return to the dorm and slip on my silk eye mask, but the night had only just begun.

"Truth or dare, Cam?" Asher asked a brunette girl with soft eyes.

"Dare," she replied with a slight grin.

"Do your best impression of . . ." Asher glanced around. "Jessie."

"I don't know. That's kinda mean." The girl bit her lip.

Chase crossed his arms. "It's a dare. You can't say no."

"Fine." She cleared her throat and began to speak in a pitchy tone, talking with her hands. "I'm Jessie, and, um . . . my favorite color is green, and—oh my goodness, is that Asher? Let me go sit next to him even though there's no space. Maybe I'll have to sit on his lap instead. How tragic. Anyway, does anyone—"

"Are you serious, Camilla?" Jessie locked her into a lethal gaze.

Camilla threaded her fingers through Jessie's hand, and Jessie slapped her away. "Oh, come on, it was just a joke. You know that I love you."

"Yeah, lighten up." Asher nudged Jessie, causing her to flinch.

"Fine. I'll *lighten* up. Suzuki, truth or dare?"

He smirked. "You know I'm a daredevil."

"Slap Camilla across the face." Jessie uttered the words apathetically. "And don't say no. After all, it's a dare."

"No way." Chase shook his head. "That's ridiculous."

"Fine, then you have to answer the truth."

"Hit me."

"Who do you like least in this room?" Jessie asked, a bitter smile playing across her lips.

Chase's face flushed. "I mean, I don't wanna be an asshole."

"Just answer," she demanded.

"Fine. She's a redhead and she just said, 'Just answer.'" Chase shrugged. "Jessie Rowley, I declare you the winner."

I tried to hold in my laughter, but most of the kids burst out in hysterics.

At once, Jessie splashed her drink in Chase's face. Liquid dripped down his cheeks. He squinted, alcohol reddening his eyes.

That's gotta be painful.

"What the hell?" Chase managed, spitting out the liquor.

"You're only proving his point, to be honest," Eric said. When he smiled, I noticed the faint gap between his two front teeth.

"Jessie, you literally forced me to answer, then got mad when I gave you the truth." Chase dried off his face with a napkin, though red blotches sprang up. "What's wrong with you?" He stood, probably to go wash up in the bathroom.

"Let's change the subject," Venus said. "Asher, I have an idea for you. Truth or dare?"

"I'll go dare." He swayed in his stupor, his heavy head swinging.

"Seven minutes in heaven. You. Bexley. Closet." A devilish grin formed on Venus's face.

My heart rate quickened. "*Venus!*" There was no use protesting with her, I had quickly learned.

She giggled.

"Truth or dare and seven minutes in heaven are two separate games," I said.

I looked to Jessie and was greeted with an expression of disgust, a scowl on her lips. Part of me pitied her; everyone seemed to treat her rudely. Perhaps she deserved it. How would I know?

I got up, leaving my imprint on the white couch. With his pretty-boy smile and a mysterious gleam to him, Asher was attractive, yes, but it didn't feel right. Still, it was a dare, and I couldn't look like a coward my first day. I had to make a go-with-the-flow first impression. After everything that had happened last year, I could withstand an awkward seven minutes of sitting in a dark room, as long as it was nothing more.

Venus led Asher's drunken sculpted body to the closet. I followed his shadow, trying to ignore the tan muscles bulging out of his tee.

Muting out the chatter and immature symphony of "do it" chants, the wooden door slammed shut, leaving me and this intoxicated stranger in the dark closet. Sleeves of old clothes and Halloween decorations tickled my shoulder.

"What's your name again?" he asked.

There was no point in telling him; he would forget it again. "Bexley. And you?"

I knew his name was Asher. But he didn't have to know that.

"Asher McCoy." He could hardly get the words out.

"Are you okay? How much did you drink?" I asked, acutely aware of how badly he reeked of alcohol.

I could barely make out his silhouette, but I saw him shrug. "Couldn't tell ya."

"Too much, that's for sure," I said.

I checked his bright watch, the only light source in the claustrophobic closet. Only one minute had passed.

Seven minutes in heaven? More like seven minutes in hell.

I fidgeted with my hair, almost thankful for the darkness. "This is awkward."

"I mean, now that you said it, yeah."

Another minute or two of complete and uncomfortable silence passed.

"Are you liking GAFTG so far?" Asher eventually asked.

"Well, classes haven't started, so I don't really know yet. I'm sure I will, though." A brief pause, and then, "What about you?"

"Eh. It's my fourth year, and I'll tell you one thing: everyone here is a snake."

"A snake? What do you mean?" I asked, not sure if I'd heard him right.

"Like, the kids here are competitive. Everyone wants to be the best."

"You mean, like, academically or socially?"

"Both. School, friends, sports, especially the elite system . . ."

"What's the elite system?" I vaguely recalled seeing those words on the website, but I hadn't looked into them.

"You don't know? Some students are selected each year, destined for greatness," he said in a mocking tone. "Don't worry. Tuffin will explain everything. All I meant was that things here can get competitive."

"What a warm welcome," I said, not trying to hide my sarcasm.

"You asked for it." Even as drunk as he was, his chortle was sweet. "At Grant, it may not be right, but you just gotta play the game. That's how you end up on top."

"Game?"

"Must be nice. To be so naive. Oblivious." He shifted in his seat. "Anyway. You know we're in here for a reason?"

"Huh?" For goodness' sake, could the time pass any slower?

"I mean, the game." He laughed. "If you don't want to, that's chill. Just tell me. Yes or no?"

No. No, no, no, no, no.

"Um, I mean, I don't know. Do *you* want to?"

Now I was *thrilled* that the room was dark; my face was practically ablaze.

"I do like to follow through on my dares. It's ultimately your choice, of course."

I could feel his heat on my cheeks, his body nearing mine, his—

"I'm so sorry."

"Did you just—"

"I'm so—" Hot chunks splattered on my cheeks, arms, clothes. "Sorry," he finished.

The closet reeked of Asher's vomit. Sour fumes assaulted my nostrils as I concentrated on not gagging. I stared down in disbelief, almost unaware of the door swinging open.

I'd rather move in, right here in the closet. Than face the embarrassment. Of being covered. In throw up.

"Looks like you two had fun in there!" someone shouted. The crowd erupted into a symphony of giggles.

My blushing was the least of my worries. Asher's partially digested who-knows-what covered every inch of my body.

"I think I'm sobered up now," he said, his eyes apologetic. Somehow, not even one trace of his puke covered *his* body.

Nasty orange and green smears were everywhere. I needed a nice long shower.

Where is Venus?

I looked around but didn't see her. Still seated, I rested my head in my hands, on the verge of tears. The thought of making eye contact with anyone in the room made me shudder. What a great way to start off the school year. Seriously, this scenario had not been included in any of my new-kid nightmares.

Within a few minutes, the spectators became either disinterested or loathed the smell and left me in complete solitude to bask in my own stink. All except for one girl whose mysterious eyes were traitors to her otherwise kind appearance. She stood with spindly limbs in a short gray dress. Her brunette hair fell to either side from a perfect middle part.

"Camilla," she said, holding out her hand for me to shake. Her nails were short and jagged, probably from biting. Her Golden bling glistened around her neck and wrists. Seemingly remembering I had previously been puked on, she withdrew her hand. "Let me help you get cleaned up."

"Really?" I asked, unsure if she was really talking to me.

"Of course, really. You're Bexley, right?"

"Yep. Weren't you at that couch playing truth or dare?"

"Unfortunately. I feel so terrible about offending Jessie. I want to apologize, but I can't seem to find her right now," she said. "By the way, don't worry about Asher. He's actually nice when he's not super out of it. On weekends, though, fifty percent of the time he's . . . distracting himself with something. Or someone," she said, rolling her eyes.

"That's too bad."

"Yeah. The stress of this place is a lot for most people. Constant assignments, papers, tests, you know. Or, you will soon." She nodded her head to the stairs. "Do you have a roommate?"

"Yeah, Venus Herrington. Do you know her?"

"Oh, I know her all right Of course I do. You're in good hands." She smirked. "Now, come on. You need a shower."

I followed her up a short staircase, music still blaring, some of the vomit shedding from my clothes with motion. I had to avoid looking at it if I didn't want to gag. At the top of the stairs, I briefly surveyed the party beneath me, gripping the rail of the balcony. Asher was laughing with his friends, as if he'd already forgotten the condition in which he'd left me. He probably had.

"Bexley? You okay?" Camilla asked, pulling me out of my thoughts.

I whipped my head around to see Camilla standing with a towel. "Yeah, I'm good. I like your jewelry, by the way."

"Thanks! The bracelet's from my brother, and the ring is thrifted." She smiled. "The bathroom is that door on the left. You'll feel better after a quick rinse." There was almost an eerie quality to her sweetness. Was she being genuine?

"Thanks so much. Really, I appreciate this more than you know," I said, taking the towel from her outstretched arms.

"Of course," Camilla said. "I'll be in the room across from the bathroom—Asher's room. He'd be fine with me chilling here. Oh, and I can handpick some clean clothes for you!"

"Don't you want to go back down? Enjoy the party?"

"Eh," she said. "Contrary to popular belief, I actually prefer the quiet. Introvert at heart. It's been a long day."

I nodded, seeing a future friend in her. "Promise?"

"Promise," she said as she turned toward Asher's room.

I smiled at her kindness, then closed and locked the bathroom door behind me and stripped my vomit-saturated clothes off. Venus's shirt was in horrid condition. Her fault for forcing me to wear it. Truly a bummer, though, was the state of my favorite pair of blue jeans. Maybe I'd be able to wash them later.

The sink was covered in a repulsive mix of shaving cream, hair, and tissues.

I twisted the shower handle and stood beneath the showerhead, recounting the previous events. My body was finally fresh, clean, renewed. Thank goodness for Camilla.

I felt severely uncomfortable in the boys' shower, so I went as fast as I could. I tried my best to ignore the gum stuck to the wall and the hairball atop the drain. Cleansing myself of Asher's puke brought a sense of serenity, but my discomfort kept me from taking my time.

It felt like around five minutes that I was in the shower, but the concept of time eluded me in my distraught condition. I got out and dried off my soaking hair and body with the towel. Camilla was probably waiting in the other room, on her phone or something. Awkwardly clad in nothing but a towel, I ditched the puke-stained clothes and scurried to the room across the hall, where Camilla was waiting. I would retrieve the clothing later.

The door was already slightly ajar.

An orange sweatshirt reading McCoy Plumbing and gray joggers lay on the navy blue comforter. "Thanks so much for getting clothes. How'd you know I love joggers?" I asked. "Camilla?"

She lay facedown, her phone faceup in her hands, but it was off, only a black screen. I was unable to see her face from where I stood. Only her tangled brown tresses. "Camilla?"

Still no response.

I tapped her shoulder and pulled it toward me, but it plopped back on the bed. Her body was heavy. Perhaps she'd fallen asleep.

She would probably want me to wake her up.

Awkwardly, I pulled on her whole body with the

upper-body strength I'd accumulated from last spring's required weight room at Vista High. Her eyes were devoid of emotion, devoid of life. Panic swelled inside me, my heart hammering in my throat.

And as my eyes trailed to her chest, I screamed. An ear-piercing, window-shattering scream.

Blood.

III

Give sorrow words; the grief that does not speak whispers the o'er-fraught heart and bids it break.
—Shakespeare, *Macbeth*

WHAT. THE. HELL.

Unblinking eyes stared back at me, a vision that would haunt me in nightmares. I heard my scream but couldn't control its growing volume.

Venus, with lipstick smeared across her chin and her cheeks, appeared by the threshold of the room. "What happened?" she asked. Her teeth chattered though it was barely cold.

Camilla's chest wasn't moving up and down. She wasn't breathing. Words couldn't come.

"Speak," she said. "What the hell happened?"

Tears of disbelief dripped down my cheeks as I stared at Camilla's lifeless body.

"What. Happ—" Venus's words cut short as she glanced in the direction of Asher's bed toward her now dead friend. She steadied herself on the doorframe, seemingly frozen in place, all the color draining from her face.

"I . . . I don't know," I stuttered.

Muffled footsteps echoed downstairs—students flee-ing the party.

"Put on some clothes, Bexley, and tell me what hap-pened," Venus demanded, her tone harsh and accusatory with an undertone of fear.

I glanced down, remembering that I was wearing only a towel, which I numbly held beneath my armpits. Asher entered his room and gasped.

"I promise I don't know." My eyes flicked to Camilla again, and I immediately wished they hadn't. Her lifeless body lay sprawled on Asher's comforter. Blood still spilled from a gash in her chest, her lips parted, her face begin-ning to drain of its once lively color.

"Take this." Asher tossed me the sweatshirt and sweatpants that had lain on his bed. There was force in his throw. Though the splatters of blood repulsed me, I wasn't going to complain.

"Thank you," I mumbled, frozen, shock setting in.

I stumbled my way to a neighboring room, went in, and shut the door to change, utter dread and disbelief coursing through me.

Venus was a couple steps behind me and flung the door open. "Bexley, explain yourself!"

I covered my body with my hands. "I'm literally not dressed, what—"

"Sorry." She turned her back to me, but her feet re-mained grounded on the floor. She clearly wasn't going anywhere. "Now explain."

I threw on the plumbing sweatshirt and sweatpants.

"You dared me, remember? To go in the closet with Asher?"

She turned back toward me, and her eyes flicked up and down. "Yeah, that rings a bell."

"And then he puked all over me. I couldn't find you, but Camilla came over and offered to take me upstairs and show me to the shower."

"Cami's the sweetest. *Was* the sweetest," Venus said, wincing as she corrected herself.

"She sat in Asher's room while I showered. Picked me out an outfit and said she didn't want to go back down to the party. She said she wanted peace and quiet for a bit." Another tear, though I'd hardly known her. "Then I walked in and saw her and screamed."

"You didn't do this." Venus's tone was almost sure, with a hint of suspicion.

"No!"

She shook her head, tears welling in her eyes. I didn't need to ask; it was obvious she'd been close with Camilla. Who would kill her?

Sirens shot through my ears, interrupting the conversation. I peered through the curtains to see blinking red lights illuminating the otherwise still and dark night. A car swiveled, skidding to a stop, and three officers raced out.

"It looks like the campus cops are here," I told Venus, reading the words marked on the side of the white car. "Someone must have called."

Venus grabbed her hair in clumps. "I can't believe this is happening."

Within moments, heavy footsteps pounded on the staircase. "Hello?" The cop's voice was gruff and assertive. I saw a sliver of the main cop's dark hair through the door. "I'm Officer Blane. I'm gonna ask you to explain what just happened," said the cop, barging into the room.

Venus, Asher, and I seemed to be the only ones left inside the house. I was too panicked to move.

"You found her? Or you saw something happen?" another officer asked.

"Found her," I squealed to the cops. Well, *cops* was a stretch; they were merely there to enforce curfews and break up parties. Now, Grant Academy's isolated address was a curse.

"Please try your best to recount the details," Officer Blane said, pulling out a notepad. "I know you're in shock right now, but just try."

I shouldn't have come to this stupid party.

A full day had passed since the calamity. A day spent hiding in my room with only a single venture to the hallway outside our room to pick up our delivered meals. Now the sun rose steadily in the sky; it was the next morning—a lovely summer day despite the darkness filling the school. The first day of September was supposed to be exciting.

Everyone gathered in the auditorium for a mandatory assembly. Grant Academy students filled rows and rows of cushioned seats, sitting as if strings were attached to the top of their heads, maintaining their stiff postures. Sniffles and soft whispers filled the room.

"Welcome, students." The woman's words echoed off the auditorium walls, which were covered in dark portraits. She looked to be in her forties; minimal wrinkles decorated the corners of her eyes, but her long dark hair appeared natural. She wore a navy blue dress that reached her feet and glasses that stood perched on her nose. Her vibe was prim yet easygoing.

"As most of you know, I'm Headmistress Tuffin. Usually, the school year's beginning is jollier than today. My sincere condolences to everyone who knew Miss Harding. She was such an outstanding student and a beautiful soul. The Academy has brought in two qualified detectives to investigate." She paused. "I encourage all of you to attend her memorial assembly tomorrow. The police are looking into the tragedy, and the criminal will be put behind bars. Classes will be postponed for a week, and we hope that students spend that time reflecting and mourning for Miss Harding." Not said but implied was the fact that the criminal presumably was among the students and faculty of GAFTG; the school was elevated on a high mountain, the nearest store miles away.

She plastered on a smile that seemed so routine I couldn't tell if it was real or fake. "For those of you returning for a second, third, or fourth year, you should know the rules. But I must emphasize them for new students and forgetful returners. Especially after the recent tragedy, it's imperative you all follow the guidelines."

Venus sat beside me, left ankle crossed over right. Her dark curls reached, gelled, to her chest. I'd expected her to nudge me and laugh at the mention of rules she most definitely wouldn't follow, but her face was solemn, not herself. Of course it was.

"After this assembly, you will all be redirected outside for the club fair, where you can sign up for extracurriculars to enrich your learning experiences.

"The first rule is coincidentally the one most broken:

no cheating. On homework, quizzes, tests—you all know this one. Depending on the seriousness, consequences can range from detention to expulsion. Secondly, girls' dorms are for girls, and boys' dorms are for boys. I hope you hear that, seniors. I believe the tragedy you all witnessed was ample punishment, but in a normal instance, such an action would entail severe consequences.

"Third, I want to address our elite system." At this, whispers traveled up and down the rows. "This is the Academy's twenty-seventh year with the system in use, and it has yielded astonishing results for our students. Of course, most of you know of this system. It's the driving motivation for many of your efforts. For the new students, the elite system refers to the three seniors elected every year in December. Essentially, three of you in each class will be chosen as 'elites' when you are seniors. These hardworking students are selected stars in and out of the classroom. They play an active role in the GAFTG community and excel in all of their subjects. GAFTG students are already set up for success, elite or not. But three of you, well, twelve of you sitting here, will have a choice at virtually any job you could ever desire, any internship, any future. Colleges and companies recognize this outstanding achievement, the best of the best. Of course, I know the Academy can be a competitive atmosphere, but I urge you not to become too cutthroat. The best students will rightfully win, and non-elites will still be plenty successful, I promise.

"I usually would not feel the need to list out the obvious rules, but it seems necessary this year. No drinking. No smoking, including e-cigarettes. No opioids, marijuana, or other drugs. No foul language, especially no derogatory curses aimed toward an individual. That covers all the big ones. In terms of more minor rules, no gum chewing and no hats indoors. And, of course, be kind to your peers. Always."

How about no murder?

"These rules are not elastic. If you are found breaking any of them, our Magistrate Board will determine your proper punishment. The seven students of the board will handle minor matters, but more serious ones will be handled by faculty, including me. On that point, resident advisor Lucas Seedly will be replaced by Jim Crawford, who's generously volunteered last minute. All boys who've been living in Beecher House will be moving into Copley House as the forensics team works in Beecher during the investigation."

Grumbles traveled up and down the rows of students. Lucas was the RA responsible for Beecher House and had gone off campus when he was on duty, during the party, hence his replacement.

"Now that that's out of the way, I ask you all to please revert your attention to the big screen, where the Grant Academy for the Gifted film will be displayed. Thank you, students. The memory of Camilla Harding will guide you through this year." It didn't feel right to hear her utter Camilla's name as something of an afterthought.

The film was the same one I'd watched on repeat at home. Now, though, it seemed boring: pretty landscapes, teacher interviews. The evergreen bow on my collar kept itching my neck. Plaid skirts and white collared tops seemed to look perfect on my classmates but hardly fit me. At least I could hide beneath my new dark buttoned suit jacket, emblazoned with a golden GAFTG crest on the chest.

The entire time, I felt the heat of many pairs of eyes. Everyone thought I had killed her. They had nothing else to believe. I was the mysterious new girl, capable of anything they'd decided. *And* I'd been the person to find her. Just my luck.

Venus trusted me. One friend.

The lights flickered back on, and the big screen rolled up into the ceiling. Headmistress Tuffin's heels clinked as she walked back to the podium in the center of the stage.

Tuffin. It was a fun name.

"Now, I invite you all out to the cobblestone commons. Please exit out any of the doors on the right." She turned off the microphone, and the students rose from their chairs in a precise, simultaneous manner. Though the school year had to begin without Camilla, a darkness seemed to engulf the student body.

Outside, booths decorated the border of the stone square. Lush grass grew through crevices in the ground. A cool breeze rustled through the cedar trees. Ping-Pong balls flew before my eyes, and students did handstands in my periphery.

"Shopping club?" Venus pointed to a black booth that had the word *Shopaholic* embroidered in neon pink.

I furrowed my brows. "There's a club for that?"

"There's a club for everything, hun." She cocked her head toward a brown table with pieces of toast popping out of toasters. "Toast club. And look, facial hair club!" Venus gestured toward a club consisting of a bunch of seniors with stubble.

"That's nice," I said dully. A student had just been murdered, and I was supposed to worry about which extracurriculars to join? It just didn't feel right.

"What do you like to do in your free time? I'll find you something," she offered, her eyes red-rimmed.

I thought about the sketchbook that lay on my new bed, filled with charcoal drawings of my innermost thoughts. The drawings weren't anything spectacular—just inner ramblings going in a thousand different directions.

As if reading my mind, Venus said, "Drawing, right?"

I nodded, brushing my thumb over the scar on my knuckle. Since last October, it had faded into nothing more than a faint mark. *Abigail loved my drawings.*

"There's an art club somewhere," Venus said, stifling a yawn. "You should join. Let's go look for the table."

She all but dragged me across the commons. I didn't understand where she was getting her energy from. The purple bags under her eyes said she hadn't been sleeping. For me, each night was different since I'd discovered Camilla's dead body. Sometimes my fatigue made it necessary to rest, and other times insomnia kept me awake into the night hours. I just couldn't erase the image of Camilla: lifeless, in a pool of her own blood.

We both put our names down for a bunch of clubs, the art club being the only one I actually planned to attend. It would be nice to finally share a passion with people who understood that drawing was more than just lines and shadows.

We both lay in our beds on opposite sides of the room. Venus was scrolling through her phone. "It's so crazy looking at old pics of me and Cam," she said, not looking up from the screen.

For a while, nothing but silence floated between us—except for the faint sounds from my diffuser, which emitted a calming scent. Still, I was far from calm. I flipped open my sketchbook and looked at the first page. I'd been so happy. Not skilled at drawing, but at least happy. Nude and pink pigments. It was a picture of a girl's mouth blowing a bubble. She almost looked like me at age thirteen, when I'd started this sketchbook.

Before Abigail.

Coming here was supposed to fix everything—ironic that half the school now thought me a murderer. How had I managed to get involved in this mess?

"I don't know what to say tomorrow," Venus admitted in a shaky voice, finally looking up from her phone.

I flinched as her voice cut through the silence. "Tomorrow?"

"The memorial assembly."

I heaved a sigh and placed my sketchbook on my nightstand. "The assembly. I didn't know you were speaking."

"Brandt asked me. Cami's brother."

"Do you have anything prepared?"

"I did. But now it sounds stupid." She sighed.

"You know the killer is among us. Has to be." She must be thinking about it too, too nervous to say the words. Maybe coming here had been a huge mistake.

There was a moment of silence. "I know," Venus said hesitantly, her voice small, laced with fear.

"You should get rest. Wouldn't want you to be a zombie tomorrow at the podium," I teased lamely.

"Don't worry. I won't. Besides, that would be better than having nothing to say." Venus yawned.

"Well, what did you have planned before?"

"It was just some bullshit about me missing her. Some superficial clichés."

I snuggled my plush purple velvet blanket. Mom had gotten it for my birthday a few years back. It even smelled like burnt cinnamon. Like home. Not like blood. Not like murder.

"Maybe something will come to you when you're up there. A little vignette is always safe. Do you have a memory of her that you think about a lot? Something that demonstrates her best traits?" I offered. "Tell a story."

The light flickered off. "Yeah. I'll do that," she whispered. "Thanks for the advice."

In my slumber, I dreamed of the very scene I was trying to forget. Finding Camilla with a bloody gash in her chest. My heart sinking to the bottom of my feet.

I tried to scream, but no sound would emerge.

I woke up, heart beating rapidly. I used to love nightmares because I could wake up and be thankful that the scenario wasn't true. But I could no longer say that.

At least today I woke up when the sun was above the horizon. I looked to find Venus sitting up in her bed, pen and paper in hand. I wondered if she'd ended up falling asleep but didn't bother asking.

"Good morning," she said, her voice ghostly. "I need to borrow a black dress. None of mine are . . . memorial appropriate."

"I can see what I have." The morning light filtered

through the blinds. My bedside clock read 9:12. The assembly began at ten.

"No need." She emerged from her covers, already dressed in my long-sleeve plain black dress. "Don't worry, you have two. I checked."

Normally, I would laugh.

"Come on. I want to get there early."

I nodded and stretched out of bed. Putting no effort into my looks, I got dressed in my short-sleeved black dress and tied my blond hair back in a bun. Camilla deserved more than a haphazard appearance, but it didn't matter. She was gone now, because of me. If she hadn't gone upstairs, none of this would've happened.

A touch of mascara on my lashes made me at least look presentable. At nine thirty, we departed and headed toward the grand hall. Mom had forced me to bring black flats, though I assured her I wouldn't wear them. But she'd been right. The old shoes were tight, toes curled uncomfortably. They reminded me of stage plays back at Vista High.

Other students filled the girls' dorm hallways, dressed drearily in black, too. Some held foundation-stained handkerchiefs; others had mascara dripping down their cheeks. Jessie shook her head when our eyes met. I wanted to snarl and yell, "I didn't do it!" But I managed a stilted smile instead. She sped ahead of us as if it hurt to see my face.

Soon, golden double doors stood before us. Venus and I entered side by side, her black heels clinking on the hardwood floor. Whispers filled the silence, most of which were probably about me. At least the people's eyes conveyed so.

A framed picture of Camilla stood, blinding. Her brown hair fell to one side, and her blissful eyes stared back at me, penetrating my soul. She wore dangling red earrings and a purple sweater.

Five minutes to ten. The long hand on the clock ticked to the eleven. The auditorium was scarcely filled, spaces separating groups of students. Venus led us to where some girls sat—her friends, probably. The stiff velvet cushions felt anything but comfortable. As we sat, the girls on Venus's right began to whisper. In unison, they rose and found a new seat.

My heart sank. They thought it was me. Everyone did.

Venus's hand trailed to mine, and I squeezed it, realizing her rapid trembling.

Headmistress Tuffin made her way from one of the front seats to the podium. Her dark hair was tied in a bun, a black lace headpiece covering her forehead. She cleared her throat. "Thank you, students, for joining us for Camilla Harding's memorial. She would've appreciated it dearly. She was such an amazing young woman.

"I hate to stand here and do this. Miss Harding wouldn't want her headmistress leading her memorial assembly. Her brother, a graduate of the Academy who flew in last night, will speak. Brandt Harding, please," she said, looking in his direction.

Brandt had dark brown hair and glasses that sat on the bump on his nose. He shared a slight resemblance with his sister—the nose and the jawline. "Thank you, Headmistress." Tuffin returned to her seat, and Brandt stood on his own, seemingly with stage fright. He was tall, so he bent over to talk into the microphone. "As a graduate of Grant Academy, I can say that this institution is not a dark place—was not, at least. This was my home for four years. I learned so much and made amazing memories. That's what school is for. Camilla came here to study, to learn, to grow. Not to be killed by one of her own peers at a party." He shook his head, disgust in his voice. "Her murderer sits among us, and they will not for long. *You* will not for long."

Eyes of many students darted to me. I looked down at my hands, interlocked in my lap. The green nail polish Mom had insisted on was chipping at the edges from my compulsive picking.

"It's no surprise that I don't excel in public speech. But I had to do this for Camilla. I love my little sister so much, and whoever did this deserves to *die*." He gazed down at a sheet of paper on the podium as murmurs from the audience answered his words. "Jessie Rowley will now speak."

Jessie stepped up, dressed in a tiny black dress that accentuated her hourglass figure—not appropriate attire for a memorial assembly.

"Camilla shouldn't have died We all know that," she began, a quiver in her voice.

What is she doing?

"But today we're not here to spread negativity. We're here to celebrate her life. A life that inspired everyone included in it. Camilla was the person who would walk into a room and make everyone smile merely due to her presence. She was such a wonderful friend, student . . . human being.

"I remember once we were running the mile in PE, and I mean, I just could not run it. Anyone who knows me knows that I'm among the most nonathletic students at the Academy. So nearly everyone was done with it, sitting on the benches by the finish line, sipping their water. It had been twelve minutes already, and I still had a lap to go. Everyone was just glad to be done with it, you know. So Camilla had finished in seven minutes, give or take, but all of a sudden, she stood up and jogged to where I was. I asked her what she was doing, though I could barely speak from the running, and she said, 'I hate running alone. Maybe you do, too?'

"Not a lot of people are like that, like her. She would do anything so selflessly, always thinking about others." I thought about how she'd helped me at the party. Not many people would've done that. "We became best friends after that. I didn't want to go anywhere that she wasn't. Camilla Harding was a ray of sunshine." The memory tugged at the corners of her mouth. "Venus Herrington will speak next."

Jessie didn't seem as terrible as she had at the party.

I nodded at Venus before she made for the front of the room.

"To be honest," Venus said, "I don't know what I'm supposed to say." She ran her fingers through her raven hair. "Camilla had the kindest heart. She was a perfect soul, too good for this world. She didn't deserve this." A tear slipped down her cheek. "*She didn't deserve this.*" Venus gritted her teeth, slamming her palm so hard on the podium that I nearly expected it to shatter. Tuffin gasped from her seat.

"Why the *hell* would someone want her to die? Huh? Why?" Her hands clawed. "I don't understand it. I don't understand how one of *you* could do this and sit here and act like everything's okay. One of you killed her. You *killed* her!"

Venus's ragged breaths caught in the microphone. So much for telling a story.

Tuffin stood from her cushion. "Miss Herrington, please take a seat."

Venus nodded, immobilized for a moment. A teacher had to escort her back to her row. When she took her seat beside me, the beads of sweat that dribbled down her face and neck were visible.

Someone else began to speak, but I wasn't listening.

"Bathroom?" Venus whispered in my ear.

I nodded and followed her out of the main room. Students gazed over at us. I avoided meeting their eyes.

The sounds of our shoes on the marble floor echoed. "Are you okay?"

"You don't need to whisper anymore." Venus wiped the sweat from her cheeks with her dress—my dress, rather, that she was borrowing. "We're out of earshot."

"Are you okay?" I repeated.

"I'm fine," she said curtly, yet everything about her appearance said otherwise. She seemed to be moments away from a full breakdown. "I shouldn't have said all those things at the podium."

"I thought that much was obvious," I blurted.

She gave a spurt of laughter, devoid of humor. "Shut up. Bathroom's right here."

Purple velvet armchairs sat in each corner, and the sink lined a long side of the wall. I plopped down on one of the chairs, and she began a staring contest with herself in the center oval mirror. We had the room to ourselves.

"Are you gonna use the bathroom?"

"No." She splashed her face with water, her mascara running. "I just needed to get out of there."

"They all think it's me," I said slowly.

"I know." She shook her head. Her hands trembled violently. "I also know that they're wrong." Venus's cheeks grew rosy, sweat accumulating.

"Venus, seriously, are you okay?"

"These happen sometimes, anxiety flare-ups. Diagnosed when I was twelve. Only happens when things are . . ." Her voice was shaky. Venus mumbled to herself, focusing. "Two things I smell: air freshener, foundation. One thing I hear: distant voices."

"Do you need anything?" I offered, feeling helpless.

"Just one."

"Of course," I said. "A towel? Some tissues?"

"Your word."

I slanted my head. "My word for . . . ?"

"We stick together and find the bastard responsible."

"I don't know. I mean, yes to the stick together part, but . . . shouldn't we leave the investigating to the professionals?"

"Just think about it," she said.

IV

Love all, trust a few,
Do wrong to none: be able for thine enemy
Rather in power than use; and keep thy friend
Under thy own life's key: be check'd for silence,
But never tax'd for speech.
—Shakespeare, *All's Well that Ends Well*

T HE CORRIDOR BUSTLED with shoulder-to-shoulder commotion as I kept my eyes on the nude-colored carpeted floor. I heaved a breath, grasping my schedule in my hands. First period was Shakespearean Literature in . . . Sodmeyer Hall. Class would begin in two minutes.

Two students descended the steps I simultaneously climbed. "Excuse me?"

They grimaced at my gaze and continued downward.

They didn't hear me.

But beneath my own lies, I knew that wasn't the case. Everyone recognized my face now, all thinking me guilty. This wasn't the type of attention I'd sought at Grant Academy.

I should've toured the campus before, identifying the locations of my classes. One minute before class wasn't the best time to find my way around—or *not* find my way around, rather. I'd wanted to explore campus last week, but all students had to stay in dorms for seven days while the cops investigated. They'd gotten nowhere thus far. During the lockdown time, however, Venus and I spent the time bonding over reality TV shows and the struggles of being the older sibling. She'd also tried to convince me to investigate with her. I just wasn't sure. Detectives were here for a reason.

The hallway sizzled down in population as the bell rang and students entered their classrooms. The crests covering each doorway read *LINDEN BUILDING*. I turned the corner to find I wasn't the last one left alone in the corridor.

Familiar red wisps immediately caught my eye. "Jessie, hey," I called out.

She smiled. Finally, someone didn't utterly despise me for the circulating gossip. Maybe I'd misread her side-eye on the way to the memorial assembly. "Are you having trouble navigating?" Jessie giggled. "I remember my freshman year, when I was new and didn't know Linden from Witz."

"Um, yeah. Would you point me in the direction of Sodmeyer?"

"Of course. You're gonna want to turn that corner and just keep walking through the bridges. You'll see a staircase at the end of the last hallway. Once you go up those stairs, you'll be in Sod."

I nodded, repeating her directions internally. "Got it. Thank you *so* much."

"Any time."

Jessie and I parted ways, and I followed the narrow corridor. The hallway was long and never-ending. I must be really tardy by now. Small marble Greek statues on podiums lined either side. My footsteps echoed as I rushed through the bridges. I breathed in dust, starting up the stairs where she'd directed me.

At the top, only one room awaited, seemingly an entire campus away from my encounter with Jessie. It must be my English classroom. The door was oddly shut with blinds closed. I knocked three times.

A teacher poked her head out with brows furrowed, inky hair swept to the side. "What are you doing here?" she asked kindly.

"Hi, um, I have Shakespearean Literature class. Sodmeyer Hall?"

The teacher laughed. "Dear, this is the teachers' lounge. You're not allowed."

"But—" I began.

"That's all right. I can walk you to Sodmeyer. It's near the other side of the campus, but I don't have anything going on right now."

Did Jessie lie to me?

I shook away the thought. Maybe I'd misinterpreted her directions or she'd slipped up.

"Oh, okay," I said, cheeks flushing. "Thank you. I would appreciate that."

In an awkward silence, she led me through endless bridges and hallways. The Academy felt like a museum, with abstract paintings catching my eye. The swirls of color could be interpreted however the viewer decided. That was one of my favorite aspects of art. I muttered the occasional "Wow" and "This painting is beautiful."

"Sodmeyer is just around here, past the statue." The teacher gestured, pointing straight ahead.

We were in the same place I'd been when I'd run into Jessie.

"Got it. Thanks again."

"Of course. Mrs. Breen, by the way. And you are . . . ?"

"Bexley Windsor. I'm new this year."

"I figured as much." She smiled. "I hope your teacher doesn't penalize you for your tardiness. Who do you have?"

I glanced down at my black-and-white schedule. "Mr. Trist?"

"Oh, sure, Trist. Well, I'm sure he'll be okay with it. Bye now."

I thanked her again before opening the door adorned with a metal number 281, corresponding to my schedule.

"So, our materials for the—" The teacher jerked his head toward me. He was a bony, rather hatchet-faced man with no hair and olive skin. "Hello, hello! Are you here for Shakespearean Literature?" he asked, his voice deep. The collar of his navy shirt stuck out the top of his gray sweater.

I nodded. The classroom was arranged with one oval wooden table, stretching from the front of the room to the back. Chairs were arranged around the perimeter of the table, and light poured through the windows.

"Please, take a seat." He ushered me toward the one empty chair. How nice; it was adjacent to Jessie. I adjusted my pleated gray skirt and sat, met with the eyes of most students, suddenly feeling self-conscious.

Jessie cleared her throat. Her red tresses were tied in a half-up, half-down hairstyle, and scarlet pigment covered her lying lips. "Class started seven minutes ago, Bexley. Where have you been?" She crossed the arms of her evergreen dress and chuckled derisively.

The truth settled over me like a rain cloud; she *had* lied to me. Tears threatened the rims of my eyes.

"No worries. Grant Academy is quite grand and hard to get around at first." At least the teacher took my side, though that probably only turned Jessie more against me.

Everyone hates the teacher's favorite.

"Anyway, Bexley, I do believe you're our only new student in the class. Would you like to come up and formally introduce yourself?"

No, no, no.

"I'm sure she would love to." Jessie.

Mr. Trist nodded at me. Clasping my hands behind my back, I sidled to the front of the classroom. From this angle, the students stared up at me with expressions of disdain.

Imagine they're all wearing underwear.

I scanned the audience for a familiar face, finding Jessie and Asher. *Asher.* His stare was less accusing than the others', though something else laced his brown-eyed gaze: confusion.

"Tell your peers about yourself. This is your chance. You have the stage." Mr. Trist smirked.

Tell them about yourself. That was the absolute worst question. What was I supposed to say? The name of my dog? My favorite ice cream flavor? My achievements?

Hi, I'm Bexley Windsor, and I'm being wrongfully accused of the murder of Camilla Harding, which I had no part in. Please don't think I'm guilty of such a disgusting crime.

Instead, I went with, "Hi, I'm Bexley, a new senior at

Grant Academy for the Gifted." I waved at the back wall dubiously. "I'm from New Jersey, and I'm . . . um . . ." I hesitated, fidgeting with my fingernails.

Mr. Trist leapt in front of me. "Okay, it seems Miss Windsor isn't a big talker. That's all right. You may take your seat," he said, gesturing to the chair beside Jessie.

I let out a breath of relief at his interruption.

"So, let's get into material for this course." Scruff lined his cheeks and chin, a brown tie upon his suit. "In contrast to the twentieth- and twenty-first-century novels you studied last year, as seniors you'll be going back in time. We'll begin by learning different literary styles and elements that will help you all construct your own work. Then we'll get into the title character, my favorite: Shakespeare himself. Depending on how long we spend with each work of literature, you all may or may not have time to work on some of your own plays. It's good stuff. Really riveting content, at least I think so."

He listed out different plays. Some of the titles rang a bell, while others were completely foreign. But the course content was the last thing currently on my mind; most students in the Academy knew me as the suspected murderer of Camilla Harding. The fact was, it could've been anyone; nobody was absolved. Venus's words echoed in my head. Yes, there were several reasons why trying to find Camilla's killer was a terrible idea, but to consider Venus's request, all I needed was one good reason: the nasty rumor to my name could be cleared. That, and justice, of course.

Toward the end of class, Mr. Trist made us answer questions that we'd "reflect on" at the end of the year: What do you look forward to most this year? What's your biggest worry? What's your favorite food? As if a year at the Academy would diminish my uncanny love for yellow peppers.

Mr. Trist had a lecture-like style of teaching, at least today. It was easy to doze off into a daydream as his hushed voice practically lulled me to sleep.

The fifty-five-minute-long class ended when a sharp bell tone pierced through my ears. Seven rings, and we were off. I could practically hear the ringing even after it had stopped.

Mr. Trist scratched his head for a moment, pondering. "Bexley, will you stay after for a moment?" Jessie muttered an "*ooh*." "Don't worry, you're not in trouble," he added.

I nodded and made for his desk as my peers filtered out of the classroom. Mr. Trist sat on a leather chair behind his tidy desk, jotting something down on a notepad. A whiteboard hung behind him.

"Bexley," he said, "I'm sorry for putting you on the spot earlier. Look, moving schools is hard, and on top of that, a few days ago a student was murdered. Gruesome."

He doesn't know they think I'm guilty, does he?

"Please, don't hesitate to reach out if you're feeling down," he continued. "In my half century of life, my most important takeaway was one thing: don't take anything personally."

I'd heard that one before. Not taking anything personally didn't change the fact that I was thought to be Camilla Harding's murderer.

"Thanks, Mr. Trist."

"Any time." He took a paper out of his desk drawer. "Oh, and take this." He handed me a map of the campus, complete with shapes and labels.

My eyes transfixed on the diagram, I exited and went down the hallway. Until—

"Ouch!" Jessie plummeted to her knees before me, binders scattering around her. Beside her stood Asher, wearing an olive-green sweater and seemingly restraining a giggle.

I hadn't even *touched* her. The whole thing was some orchestrated act.

"Here, I'll help," I said, bending down to gather stray papers.

"No, get away!" Jessie shouted. "I don't want your bloodstained hands anywhere near my materials." Her eyes moved to Asher. "Will you help me?"

Asher and I made short eye contact, though he shook out of it after a moment. "Yeah, of course," he said.

Jessie watched me with an evil death stare, as if willing me to leave.

So I did.

"Wait!" Asher jutted out his arm to stop me. "Bexley."

"What are you doing?" Jessie snorted.

He jogged a few meters to catch up with me, some of Jessie's papers arranged in his arms. In a whispery tone inaudible to Jessie, he said, "I'm sorry. About throwing up and making a mess all over you. I know Camilla came to help you, and I know you were in the shower when it happened. You don't deserve this blame." He sounded genuine.

I shrugged. "That's nice, but you're one person. Everyone else thinks I did it."

"Jessie's not everyone." He shook his head, a lock of brown hair falling over his eye. "To be honest, I don't even know if she truly thinks it's you or if she just wants someone to blame. And who better to blame than the person who spent seven minutes in a closet with her crush?"

So he has an ego, and not a small one.

"Asher, stop talking to that bitch!" Jessie yelped, her papers fully gathered. "She kills people who are nice to her."

Facing me, Asher rolled his eyes. And walked back to her.

But how does Jessie know Camilla was nice to me?

"How was English?" Venus, enjoying her free period, looked up from her computer screen as I entered our room. She wore purple sweatpants, a black cropped tank, and had her curls tied atop her head. The sunlight streamed through the windows directly at my face, practically blinding me. "Your bed is more comfortable, by the way."

I laughed and joined her atop my comforter.

"Terrible," I admitted, rubbing my temples. I felt the beginning of a headache forming, and it was only morning.

"Really? Why? I've heard Mr. Trist is one of the best teachers."

I shook my head. "It's not him, it's—"

"Oh, no. Who's in your class?" she interrupted.

"Jessie. And Asher, but most importantly, Jessie." I picked at a loose string on my comforter.

"Yeah, she can be—Didn't I warn you about her at the party?"

"Yeah. She seemed so genuine and caring at the memorial assembly, though."

"Key word, *seemed*. It's all a facade, I'm telling you. Jessie's about as fake as the school chicken nuggets." Venus shrugged. "Besides, feeling down about her best friend's murder doesn't make her a saint."

"True. You know . . . She seemed really pissed at Camilla at the party."

"Yeah, she's always pissed about *something*. But she was sitting in that cluster of friends the entire night. She couldn't have."

"Yeah, I guess." Something about that explanation didn't seem right, though. Hadn't Camilla said she couldn't find Jessie when she'd wanted to apologize?

"Late breakfast?" Venus proposed, shutting her laptop.

"Food seems like a good idea."

"I'm impressed you found your way back to the dorm after class. Sodmeyer is kind of on the other side of campus."

I held up the diagram. "Courtesy of Mr. Trist."

"Nice." Venus stretched out of bed. "Come on, I'm famished. Did you just hear my stomach?"

Gilded double doors enclosed the dining hall from the front entrance, embellished with the school mascot: a golden eagle. A Gifted Golden Eagle.

The dining hall had been closed off for safety precautions following Camilla's murder. Little by little, GAFTG was reopening community spaces. Long rectangular tables filled the vast space, decked out in polished wood. Painted portraits of men and women covered the walls—some familiar faces.

"Famous alumni," Venus said, watching me stand in awe of the painted works. Venus pointed from table to table. "Tea station, hot breakfast, baked goods, oatmeal station, omelet bar . . . There are more, too. Take your pick."

My eyes widened, taking it all in. Vista didn't serve breakfast, but for lunch, they had one hot lunch option, usually a grotesque concoction of melted cheese and some meat that came from who-knows-where. Here, the worst aspect of dining would be not knowing what to choose.

The line out the door for the omelet bar nearly steered me away, but the omelets looked too good to ignore. Amidst foreign faces, Venus and I stood and waited.

I broke the silence. "I can't believe classes are starting up like everything's normal."

"I know." Venus shook her head. "She deserves more than a week off classes. Aren't you glad that school's starting, though?"

A sense of normalcy would at least be a distraction. "Yeah, I guess. I just wish it didn't have to be like this."

"You're not alone there. This sucks. Your year is supposed to be thrilling. Instead, it's being plagued with . . . this."

"Yeah. It's more important than just my year, though. Think about her family." I didn't want to cry anymore; I'd done it enough in the past week. "It kills me that while I was worrying about hairballs in the boys' bathroom, she was . . ." That familiar golf ball lump was forming in my throat again.

"It doesn't make sense. Why her? Why Camilla? She was perfect. They could've taken anyone else." Her voice broke after the word *perfect*. "We'll find out soon," she said, adding the word "together" as she looked me in the eye, hopeful.

I peered out around the engraved metal windowpanes to find a striking tree with pink flowers. "I don't know." After how Jessie had treated me, all I wanted was to lift the blame. Still, there was a part of me that didn't want to further risk my reputation or do anything to jeopardize my year at Grant.

"Egg whites with spinach and parmesan, please," I said. The line had gone by faster than I'd anticipated.

I watched the omelet man do his magic, sprinkling cheese and spreading out spinach on a bed of white fluff. Afterwards, he flopped the breakfast onto a plate and handed it to me with food-stained white gloves.

Waiting for Venus's omelet to be ready, I explored the tables of the dining hall, especially attracted to the tea station. A box split into sixteen different compartments— two by eight—sat on the wooden table. Each had a different type of tea bag. Pomegranate, chai, peppermint . . .

A hand reached into the green tea box beside me: that of a man, looking to be between the age of a graduate and a teacher.

"What are you looking at?" the man said curtly, cutting into my thoughts.

I flicked my gaze off him, looking to my left and right, wondering to whom he was talking.

Oh, me.

"Pardon?"

"Quit staring." He rolled his eyes. "I know I look a mess right now."

His voice was familiar; I'd heard it before.

Of course.

He was Camilla's brother, Brandt, who'd spoken at the memorial. "Sorry. For staring, and for your loss."

"Okay."

For the record, he looked far from a mess. His dark hair was gently slicked back, parting off-center. His circular lenses angled downward over his aquiline nose.

I probably should've stopped talking, but curiosity got the best of me. "Are you staying here? At the Academy, I mean."

"Nah. I'm staying at a nearby hotel. I'm close with the faculty here, though. They allowed me to hang out and eat on campus. I'm a graduate. They either like me or feel bad for me, but either way, it works to my benefit."

"Nice."

"Nice?" He grimaced. "I'm here to find out who killed my sister. *Nice* isn't exactly the word I would use."

"Right. I'm so sorry, I . . ." *Don't know what else to say.*

"It's whatever. No one knows how to act around people who are suffering from grief. I've learned that in the past few days."

"You're right about that. Communication is one of the hardest parts. Everyone expects you to explain how you're feeling, as if you could so easily put it into words, and—sorry, I should stop blabbing. I'm Bexley, by the way."

"No, no, you're right," said Brandt. He bit the inside of his cheek.

Neither of us spoke, but clitters and clatters of silver-ware and indistinct chatter filled the dining hall. I picked out a cinnamon tea bag.

"So are your parents here, too?" I asked to fill the silence.

"Nah. They told me it was stupid to stay here. I mean, objectively, I guess it is." He looked somewhere in the distance, seemingly deep in thought.

"Have you graduated college?"

"Graduated last year. Now I've just been searching for jobs. The sad thing is that Camilla wouldn't have had to."

"Wouldn't have had to search for jobs? Why?" Steam evaporated from my mug as I gently placed in the tea bag.

"Are you not in her grade? Everyone knows that she was perfectly on track to be an elite." He shook his head. "Now some son of a . . . Someone fucked that up."

Camilla would have probably been an elite . . .

"Anyway, I'm really not supposed to share anything about the investigation or be investigating at all, for that matter, but I gotta go talk to those elite runners-up. At this school, people are cutthroat."

I dropped a sugar cube into my mug. "Are you suggesting they . . . take the term literally?" I shivered as the realization set in: someone at school had a motive.

"Bexley!" Venus approached me, plate in hand. "There you are."

I beckoned her toward me at the tea station, ready to introduce Brandt, but when I looked to my right, he was gone.

V

Reputation is an idle and most false imposition;
Oft got without merit and lost without deserving.
—Shakespeare, *Othello*

HANGING LIGHTS HOVERED over each table,
gilded with fleur-de-lis and jewels. The cavernous library was flanked with mahogany pillars in each of the four
corners and smelled of old books. Endless brown shelves
lined the walls, filled with rows and rows of leather-bound
books.

"Come on." Venus pulled me from my trance of ad-
miration, pointing toward a corner of the room.

The table she led me to was tucked away. Before us sat
four long windows. The translucent pearl color muted the
outside greenery.

Aside from my horrid English experience, the two
other classes I'd had so far went all right. In both Latin
and history, the teachers simply ran through the year's materials and introduced themselves.

The clock read a quarter to noon; I had calculus in

fifteen minutes. And, to my dismay, Mr. Bates was the name on my schedule—that awkward teacher who'd shown me around on my first day.

Before it all went downhill.

I dropped my bag on the wooden floor, and the sound echoed in the quiet room. After what Brandt had suggested about potential motives, how Jessie had been treating me, and how everyone suspected me, investigating seemed like the only option. "We need to talk to the elite runners-up."

Venus squeaked. "So you're in?"

"I'm in, and we gotta talk to the elite runner-ups."

She smiled. "I know." Venus pulled her phone from her pocket and fixed her ponytail as she examined herself on selfie mode. "So what were you talking about with Brandt Harding?"

"That."

"I see."

"He's staying here to investigate," I said.

"They don't release the elite list until December, but a lot of people are . . . predictable," Venus said with an air of mystery.

"Like who?" Maybe finding suspects would be easier than I had thought.

"Out of the people I'm friends with, I know Eric and Chase were in the running. There are a bunch of other smart kids, though—those are just the people I talk to." Venus pursed her lips. "And, of course, Camilla. She was perfect in *everything*."

"She didn't deserve this."

"No. Of course she didn't." She gave a plaintive sigh. "Camilla was the type of person who was easy to get jealous of. She was an outstanding student, well loved in every social circle, and scored more goals in one soccer game than most could hope to score in a season." She paused. "Once you got to know her and became close with her, the envy vanished. It became a desire—to study with her, to be around her, to be her best friend." Venus bit the inside of her cheek. "She was my person. You know, the person who understands you better than you understand yourself? She opened my eyes to a lot of things that, when I think about them now, would've maybe . . . been better left unseen." Her gaze drifted toward the wall of windows ahead.

Not sure what to say, I smiled sympathetically as the clock's long hand ticked to the ten. "I'd better get going to calculus. Care to show me the way?"

Mr. Trist's diagram would have been satisfactory, but I'd rather not walk alone. And there was potentially a murderer on the loose. Despite my layers and being indoors, a shiver traveled down my spine.

"Sure." Venus led me out of the library, her ponytail swinging side to side with each stride.

On the walk through the corridors, she said, "I don't think Eric or Chase would ever even think to hurt Camilla. Everybody loved her, especially Chase."

"Loved her?"

Venus laughed. "Goodness, not like that. I just meant that Chase was one of Camilla's closest friends. Even if they were jealous, would that really drive them to murder her? No, it's gotta be bigger than that," she said convincingly.

"In any case, they're all we have right now. They might be a good starting point."

"True." Venus nodded as we turned the corner. "I'll text them. You and I can meet with them during leisure time. Sound good?"

I glanced down at my schedule to find the block of free time from four to six, then remembered how the art club scheduled their first meeting in that block. Oh, well. The club could wait. "Perfect."

Venus halted our walk at a door, outside which many students gathered. "See ya then. Well, at lunch next period, too, but also then."

I waved my goodbye as Mr. Bates swung the door open. "Welcome!" he sang, dark hair neatly gelled. "People, take your seats please." His British voice fell somewhere between strict and jolly. "Oh, I know you!" he said, smirking as I entered. "Sit anywhere you'd like for today, people." Individual desks were set in rows. I scanned the room for a familiar face and found none. Something in me was thankful for the fact.

He dimmed the lights and projected on his board a picture of an attractive adolescent boy that looked around my age. As the crowd settled into chairs behind individual desks, he asked, "Does anyone know who this is?"

This isn't history or English class.

"No? I expected as much." Mr. Bates cleared his throat. "This is David. David Bates. Also known as your calculus professor, when he was your age."

I held in a bit of laughter.

"That's right. Contrary to popular belief, I was, in fact, a teenager once. Long ago, when dinosaurs roamed the Earth. Ancient times, really, but it happened nonetheless." He tugged on his olive-green tie. "You might think I'm a bit mad. But too often students think teachers are only teachers. Or that teachers are simply an embodiment of facts and exams. But I'm a real person, with a real life. Anyway, enough of that, let's get to some calc. That's why you're all here, right?"

He projected a mishmash of numbers and symbols on the board. I settled in for what was going to be a long class.

"Have the police talked to yet?" I asked Venus.

"Early today, actually." She paused. "My alibi seemed to satisfy them, so they're off my back now." I was about to ask what exactly her alibi was when Chase's tall silhouette appeared in the distance.

"You wanted to talk to me?" He approached, his denim backpack hanging off one shoulder. "Whoa. You guys look extremely intimidating right now."

The fall air smelled fresh. Venus and I leaned on the trunk of a tree, close to an Academy turret building. I wondered how anybody found their way around the vast campus. Venus had guided me here. My fingers sat in my lap, interlaced. My face was stern.

"Hey, I kinda remember you." His eyes narrowed at me as he dropped his sweatshirt atop the grass to sit on. "I was also kinda wasted. Bexley, right?"

"Yep."

We sat in an isolated area, away from the rest of the campus and the world. Venus patted the grass, encouraging him to sit. "Come on. You're seven minutes late to our meeting."

"Chill out. I just got released from *Français Quatre*. Besides, we're free for like two hours," he protested.

"No can do. We have our next meeting at four thirty. Twenty-three minutes from now," Venus said. "Sit your ass down."

"Jeez, official. Who's your next meeting with, or is it, like, confidential?" he said, finally dropping to the ground and sitting in front of us.

"The latter," Venus said flatly.

"Anyway, you wanted to talk about Camilla?" Chase ran his fingers through his inky hair, rolling his eyes.

I nodded. "We think you might know something."

"*Me?*" Chase chuckled. "Ironic, as people seem to think *you're* the guilty one here."

My fists clenched by the sides of my houndstooth skirt. So many curses came to mind, but I restrained myself.

"Suzuki, first of all, stop. Second, we never said we thought you killed Cami. We said we think you might know something." Venus placed a lined sheet of paper onto her clipboard. "There's a difference."

"Fine. So what do you suggest I know?" Annoyance laced his words.

Venus and I exchanged unknowing glances; we hadn't prepared much.

"Please share any potential suspects," ordered Venus.

"I really don't know much." Chase scratched his hair. "Between you and me, the brother's a little sus. He, like, interrogated me today," he said, brow furrowed.

The brother? Brandt?

Ballpoint pen in hand, I scribbled down his name.

"Whoa, whoa, whoa, what are you writing? I said between *us*." He started to go red.

Chase reached out to my clipboard, but I angled it more toward me, shielding the paper from him. "Just a doodle."

"Hold up." Venus arched a brow. "How is he suspicious? Brandt Harding? Why would he do anything to harm his own sister?"

Chase put both hands up in the air. "Never said he would. The fellow seems off to me, that's all." He lingered on the word *off*.

Venus sighed. "Let's move on. You and Cami were always together. Did you ever notice anything . . . odd about her?"

"Huh?" Chase shrugged. "Venus, you were around her more than I was. You would know more than me."

"Just answer the question, Suzuki," Venus said, unwavering.

"No, I mean . . . The only class we shared last year was calc. That was the only time I ever saw her in classes. Then, of course, we studied together and hung out on weekends, but . . ." *But what?* "I don't know, never mind."

"Say it," Venus and I said in unison.

"No, nothing. All I was gonna say was that . . . Camilla was perfect at everything. Almost too perfect. She seemed to ace even the hardest tests, especially in math. Her grades were always flawless—so much as a regular A instead of an A-plus didn't often, if at all, show up on her report card."

"Yeah, she was gifted." Venus crossed her arms. "What are you saying? You think she cheated?" Redness filled Venus's cheeks, as if she were defensive on Camilla's behalf.

"Chill." Chase laughed. "I will neither confirm nor deny."

As Venus opened her mouth, two teachers came out of the turret building beside us. She held her tongue for a moment, waiting for our isolation to return.

Chase plucked blades of grass from the ground beneath him. "Hey, what happens in the teachers' lounge stays in the teachers' lounge," he said, eyes following the two teachers.

"I think you said that a little too loud," Venus said once the faculty had passed.

"Can we be done? Obviously you guys know more than me. And even what I do say, you don't seem to believe, *Venus*." Chase swung his backpack over his shoulder and stood, his flippant tone increasingly irritating by the second.

"Fine. You're dismissed." Venus shooed him away with her hand as if he were a pestering fly.

Wiping the grass off the bum of his gray joggers, he shifted his playful gaze toward me. "By the way, Bexley, Asher may or may not have talked about you. To me," he said coyly, a grin spreading across his face.

"Oh my goodness, Bexley!" Venus's eyes sprang alive. "Define 'talked about.'"

"Jeez, I shouldn't have said anything. He'd kill me if he found out I mentioned it."

"I wouldn't be throwing around the word *kill* these days. And come on, Suzuki"—Venus smirked—"you know I'm great with secrets." She gave him a playful wink.

"Are you forgetting last year?" he said.

A crinkle formed between Venus's brows as she became deep in thought. "Last year . . . Last year . . . What was last year?"

"You. Principal. Busted. Me. Weed."

"Oh, that. Well, yes, that rings a bell." She shook her head. "But that was one time. Besides, they said if I didn't speak up, I'd be the one to get in trouble. I couldn't lose my position on the Magistrate Board."

"Whatever."

"Yeah, whatever. You were able to erase the whole thing with Daddy's money. And anyway, I don't need you to tell me more. It's obvious Asher has the hots for Bexley." Venus laughed. "Sexy Bexley. It rhymes! Has anyone ever called you that?" she said, turning to look at me.

My cheeks flushed. "No."

"Stop it, you're embarrassing the new girl," Chase said. "Enjoy your next confidential meeting." He put up air quotes as he said *confidential*. "See ya."

As he escaped from my vision, I turned to Venus. "Great. We gained absolutely *nothing* from that."

"Eh, we gained some gossip about Asher." She shook my shoulders. "You know, he's not a bad option. And just imagine how Jessie would feel."

"Please, don't make this about Jessie."

"Sorry. Of course it's not about her." She gave a sly smile. "It's just an added bonus." Venus pulled her phone out and began typing.

"What'cha doing?" I asked, trying to get a glimpse of her screen.

She raised her eyebrows up and down. "Nothing."

"Tell me!"

"And, send." A whoosh noise sounded from her phone. "Asher now has your number."

"Venus!"

"You'll thank me later." She patted me on the shoulder, but I shook from her grip, not sure how to feel about all this.

Why would Asher talk about me to Chase? And what type of talking was it?

"In other news, Eric should be arriving in a bit."

As if on cue, Eric materialized, emerging from the shadow of a tree a medium distance before us. His blond curls ended just above his curious blue-green eyes. He walked unconfidently, each step hesitant.

"Hey, Eric!" Venus waved frantically at him, as if we were otherwise invisible.

He jogged over to us. "Hey, Venus. Hey, Bexley Windsor."

Who does he think he is, calling me by my full name?

Venus managed a smile, and I couldn't decipher whether it was genuine. "You're early."

He stretched his arms before taking a seat. The information Venus had told me about him flooded to mind: his celebrity parents and the way his friends tolerated him solely because of them.

Eric placed his unzipped bag on his lap. A banana, a binder, and a blade poked out.

"Sorry, ceramics class," he said, regarding the knife and the look of apprehension that must've been painted across my face. "I'm just taking it for the required art credit."

Venus pursed her lips. "Oof, good luck. Mrs. Garrett?"

"How'd you know?"

"I had to take that hell of a class last year." Venus chuckled, seemingly reminiscing. "Oh, she and her pastel sundresses. It was the worst, but Camilla and I had each other. She made it the class I looked forward to the most." Venus blinked away the memory, leaving remnants in the form of wet droplets by her eyes. "Anyway, do you have anything you can tell us about Camilla?"

Eric wore a brown knit sweater layered over a collared shirt. He fidgeted with an unraveling thread on the sleeve. "Why would I know anything about her? Little Miss Perfect wouldn't want to waste her precious time hanging out with me, so no. Weren't you, like, one of her best friends?"

"Hey!" The lethal tone in her voice petrified even me. "*Don't* disrespect Camilla like that."

"I didn't mean any disrespect." Eric rolled his eyes, the motion contradicting his semi-apology. "I just meant that we were only associated because our friend groups were. But the two of us hardly had a relationship. We both did golf in the spring. That's all."

"Whatever." Venus wiped beneath her eyes. If there was a tear, she clearly wanted to get rid of it before we would notice. "Kindly excuse yourself, please."

"So you made me walk all the way here just to talk for less than a min—"

"You heard her." My own assertion startled me. "I mean, she asked you to leave, kindly."

Eric crinkled up his face and sauntered off.

"Venus, I understand he's annoying, but we could've missed something valid that he was gonna say." I glanced down at the paper on my clipboard, empty save for the name *Brandt Harding*. "We got nothing from that. But hey, this interrogation is gonna be a marathon, not a sprint." I sighed. "Venus?"

I looked over to find her hugging her knees, her chin curled into her chest. Her body shook, small movements.

"Are you okay?" But it was a stupid question.

She looked up at me with red-rimmed eyes, mascara streaking down her face. "I just miss her."

I wished I could help in some way, but it was impossible. Camilla was gone, and I couldn't reverse her tragic fate. So I did what I could: I comforted her. "Time heals all wounds. That's what my mom always says." I cringed at how old I sounded. It was a phrase Mom often offered. There was, however, some truth to it; time helped me forget about Abigail. At least a little bit.

As I stroked Venus's back in gentle motions, my phone rang with a sharp beep, startling me. It was a text message from an unknown number.

> Hey, I think we shld get together
> and talk sometime. If u want.

My stomach fluttered. The device beeped a second time.

> This is Asher btw. McCoy.

VI

Who ever loved, that loved not at first sight?
—Shakespeare, *As You Like It*

"UTTERLY STUNNING." VENUS stood before me, staring me up and down. "I cannot believe this is happening."

"Relax, nothing is *happening*." The face that blinked back at me was hardly my own; blue pigment lined my waterlines, my lips covered with matte red. Silky pink fabric draped down my body. "Who is she?"

"Huh?"

I pointed to the girl in the mirror. "Her."

"You look gorgeous." Venus smiled. "I'm gonna head to the library, but when you get back tonight, you're telling me every detail."

"Will do. And it's not a date!" I yelled as she slipped out the door, leaving me alone before the mirror.

Out of instinct, I grabbed a tissue and wiped off the maroon lipstick. After seven tissues, I figured a light stain would be the best I would get. Venus and I couldn't be more different, and I loved it about her.

Should I change the dress?

Amidst my contemplations, my phone buzzed:

Asher

Meet by the dining hall doors in five?

Five minutes would barely be enough time to get there, let alone change first.

Asher

There's a cool place on campus I can show you.

Empty-handed save for my phone, I exited through the doorway in high-top sneakers. The dining hall was one place I could find, thank goodness. My breathing quick, I walked the wooden hallways, mostly empty except for a few students wandering after their second day of classes. Why was I so nervous? For the date, or because I was standing alone in a school at which a murder had recently taken place? This wasn't a date. It was just . . . What was it just?

The dining hall's familiar gilded double doors came into view. The grandfather clock adjacent ticked to seven o'clock. Nobody was here.

I was debated typing a text to Asher when his footsteps entered earshot.

"Bexley." His voice trembled nervously. "I was worried you wouldn't come." His caramel hair parted in the middle, waves curling over his ears. I could see how any girl could get lost in his eyes—pupils of sweet intent riddled with corruption. He held a washed-out leather-bound book in one hand and his phone in the other.

"What's that you're holding?" I asked. Uneven stitches covered the spine.

"Come on, I want to bring you someplace."

"Where?"

His lips curved into an innocent smirk. "Walk with me."

I stepped to his side, observing a slight sheen of sweat on his face. In a strange way, knowing of his nerves eased my own.

"I need to apologize," Asher began.

"For?"

"Everything." We passed clay and marble statues of faces on stands in the corridor. "The party. Jessie. You don't deserve any of this."

"That's all right," I said eventually, not totally believing the words as they left my mouth.

"It's not, though." Asher stopped walking and turned to me. I observed his handsome outfit: a sweater and kha-kis with a tweed overcoat—a far cry from the joggers and T-shirt he'd worn at the party. Perhaps my dress wasn't too much after all.

"I know it's not. But what's done is done," I said.

I followed him down the halls, trusting the certain look on his face.

"Where are we going?"

"Almost there."

I nodded. "Why do you hang around with Jessie?" The question was a bold one, yet he didn't seem too startled at my ask.

"Jessie is complicated." He shrugged. "The way she's

treated you isn't okay. But it's because of Camilla, I think. She wants to blame someone, and you're, well, right there."

As we ambled closely, his fingers brushed against mine. I couldn't tell if the motion was accidental. Either way, I relished in the ephemeral sensation it gave, stirring within me. My rational side hated the effect this boy—almost stranger—had on me.

"We're here," Asher announced.

"Here?" I asked. Before us was a doorway, cobwebs decorating the knob.

"My favorite place." He smiled, his single dimple adorable. "Come."

Into a bug-infested room?

"Trust me," he said, his tone reassuring.

Legs wobbly, I followed behind him. Asher wiped the webs off the knob and held the door for me.

"This?" Dust covered the seats of scattered chairs, and cobwebs draped over the cushions. "The place you wanted to show me?" I asked, suppressing a cough.

On the far side of the room was a pearly door to the outside. He made for the handle and swung it open. "This," he said, "is the place."

The door led to a wide balcony with a ground of cobblestone and walls that reached my hips.

"I'll be right back." Asher escaped into the room, then returned a few moments later with two chairs in hand. He placed them beside each other and wiped off the cobwebs. He sat down and gestured to the second chair. Dust piled on the ground, dirtying my shoe bottoms. "Sit?"

Purples and blues filled the sky, surrounding the setting circle of light. "It's nice to watch the sunset from here," I said.

My gaze was fixed on the sky, but I felt his eyes on me. "Yeah, and no one ever really comes here, so we don't need to worry about people eavesdropping . . . not like that . . . I mean like . . . If we were talking about something we didn't want . . . I'll just shut up now." Melodies came from his phone: a harmony of strings and keys. "I should've brought a speaker."

I couldn't help but giggle as I fidgeted with the hair that framed my face. "It's okay."

Asher hummed over the music. "I've made a terrible first impression, haven't I?"

"You mean at the party?"

"The closet, the vomit, the circumstance . . . everything about that night. It shouldn't have happened." He sighed. "If I could erase one night of my life, it would be that one."

"Were you close with Camilla?"

"Yes." He didn't elaborate, and I didn't pry.

"I'm sorry."

"Me, too."

"Who do you think did it? Someone who wanted to be an elite?" A loud silence floated between us. "Or Jessie. She seemed mad at Camilla after the whole impression thing and truth or dare."

He paused. "The notebook."

"Didn't know an inanimate object was capable of murder, but—"

He handed me his leather book. The pages bulked the book so that the cover existed at an upward angle. My mind filled with speculations as I flipped open the cover. What mysteries could be contained within these sheets?

"She deserves justice. And justice will always prevail," Asher said. "And by the way, Jessie wouldn't kill her best friend over some petty impression."

A first and last name covered each page—each page out of over one hundred. Below each name were bullet points.

In her chemistry class and on the soccer team, never as good as her.

"What is this?"

"Every student in our grade. And the relevant ones in other grades." Asher shook his head. "I need to find out who did this."

Questions bloomed in my head, though they weren't the ones that I should've been thinking.

Did he invite me here just to investigate Camilla's murder? Or was it for other reasons, like Chase hinted?

Now that he had showed me the suspect-filled journal, it must've been the former. Besides, I could've over-thought Chase's words.

"Venus and I are trying to find the killer, too," I finally said.

"I know. I was gonna suggest . . . I don't know, maybe we could try to figure this out together. I mean, if that's all right with you and Venus. I really care about finding Cami justice."

My mind blanked, and only one word came out of my mouth. "Yes."

So that was the reason he wanted to "talk." A shameful feeling gripped my gut. It shouldn't have annoyed me; he wanted to lock up Camilla's murderer, as did I. But maybe that wasn't what I'd expected of the night, if I was being honest with myself.

He shrugged. "Nothing in there is useful. Losing a soccer game against Camilla wouldn't be a proper motive to kill her, at least for a sane person."

"Maybe it wasn't someone at the Academy," I suggested, though I was nearly sure that the culprit resided within these isolated New Hampshire walls.

"Unlikely, but possible," he said.

"I hate that school isn't releasing any information. Like, the murder weapon and all that. Do you have any idea about . . . ?"

Asher shook his head and exaggerated a heavy breath. After a short silence, he muttered, "Suzuki told me that you and Venus talked to him today."

"Yeah. We gained nothing from it, though," I said.

"Why did you decide to come here, to the Academy, Bexley?" Asher asked, turning sideways to face me.

"Pardon?" I'd heard him, though the sudden change of subject was a surprise. I fidgeted with the hem of my dress.

"Why the Academy? And why senior year?" he pressed.

"I don't know," I lied. "I guess I wanted to get away. It's ironic, though, because now I know what wanting to get away really feels like. No offense to you, or any of the students, but I can hardly walk to a class without someone whispering about me to a friend, or at the very least shooting me a nasty glare." There was at least a bit of truth to my words.

"I'm sorry." He'd said the two words too many times. "Did you hate me after I threw up on you?"

"Hate is a strong word." I grinned until I remembered the larger incident that had followed the trivial one. "I certainly wasn't content with you." I moved a flyaway hair

from my eyes. "Okay, maybe I hated you. You're gonna have to win me over somehow."

"Hmm." He smiled again, showing that annoyingly adorable dimple. "I'll find a way."

The classical song that played on his phone segued into the next. This one made my head busy, alternating between two notes that frequently switched.

"Sound familiar?"

"A bit."

"It's the prelude to Bach's Cello Suite in G." Asher hummed the melody, anticipating the notes that came next.

"So, you're a sucker for classical music, huh?"

He placed his index finger over his mouth. "Shh."

"Why would you want to conceal the best part of you?" We engaged in an unannounced staring contest, our pupils separated by a few feet, simultaneously connected.

"I'm not concealing anything from anyone. I play classical music on the piano for my family all the time." He blinked first. "I just have different faces that I choose to wear at different times."

"So you're pretty much admitting that you're two-faced?"

"Yeah," he said. "And before you criticize that, don't claim you aren't the same. Unpopular opinion: everyone is."

"I don't think that's true," I quickly retorted.

"So you're saying you could act in front of your parents the same way you act in front of your friends? You wouldn't feel weird doing that?" he said, eyes narrowing.

"That's completely different."

He shrugged. "I don't know. Seems the same to me."

"Fine." I began in a mocking tone, "Academia Asher

wears tweed overcoats and listens to strings, and the other Asher drinks himself into a stupor on weekends and likes Jessie?"

"Neither of the Ashers *like* Jessie. You know, the teachers often mistake her rudeness for wit." The music picked up in pace, becoming more intense.

"Mm-hmm." I paused. "That's cool that you play piano. You'll have to show me sometime."

"Okay, but I'm not that good." He bit his lip. "Don't have high expectations."

"That's what the prodigies always say." I smirked.

"Fine, then I'm amazing. There is no one better than me."

"That's what the prodigies with big egos say."

"Okay, so what do the people who actually aren't good say?" He grinned. "I got you stumped."

"Oh, well." I shrugged contently. "Do the two Ashers have anything in common?"

"Uh . . . brown hair? They're both only children. And their mother is a lawyer, and their father owns a plumbing company, which both Ashers' friends like to joke about."

"I see. That makes sense considering the McCoy Plumbing clothes you lent me."

The bottom of the sun began to disappear beneath the horizon. "Let's not think about that night." If he didn't want to think about it, perhaps it hadn't been his only intention in asking me here.

"Sure." Suddenly I thought back to when the band of his joggers was around my waist, a forbidden memory to reminisce about. "That clothing was eerily comfortable nonetheless."

"I have more where those came from." His cheeks

turned a dark shade of red, though a smile crept onto his lips. "Has anyone ever told you that you have cool eyes?"

Butterflies fluttered in my stomach.

"They're like crystals. I fear that if I stare too long, I'll turn into stone."

"Don't worry." I pursed my lips and shifted in my chair. "Medusa's eyes are green in most stories." The song was over, replaced with a more hopeful tune. "Speaking of snakes, I keep thinking about what you told me."

"What I told you?"

"At the party. You said everyone here was a snake." Saying the words, I was brought back to that night: the dark closet, the truth or dare, the puke. "You said that before Camilla was . . ."

"And it stands true after—especially after." He tapped on his phone to check a notification. "How can one listen to this song and not dance? It gives me a sudden urge to get on my feet and sway." He ruffled his hair with his hands and met my gaze. Was he implying what it seemed? "'Waltz of the Flowers,' Tchaikovsky."

Arm outstretched, he bent before me, satirically bowing his head. His calloused hand inches from mine, I observed every curve and crevice. Gently, I placed my fingers in his, chuckling.

What is going on?

I pushed down the giddy energy that begged to spill out.

Act coy. Act as if you've been asked to dance before.

Our fingers interlocked, we waltzed around the cobblestone balcony. I followed his lead and quickly got the hang of it. Asher bobbed his head to the rhythm, emphasizing each third beat. More instruments joined the symphony, and we erupted into laughter. My self-consciousness frequently made me cover my mouth with my palm when I laughed, but tonight there was no need. Even if I tried, my hands were cupped in his. I allowed myself to simultaneously let go and hold tighter.

He smiled so widely that every one of his perfect teeth gleamed. The sun faded away, and stars began to illuminate the night like polka dots. I imagined the dusty ground as a checkered ballroom floor, the lamp beside us as a sparkling chandelier. My pink silk dress could be a gown with endless layers of tulle, his tweed coat an embroidered royal tunic.

Our hands were the only parts of us that touched. He twirled me in and out with his bare fingers, which I imagined were covered with lustrous yellow satin gloves. We continued to dance until the song faded out, lingering for a few moments.

"We'll be seeing each other more often." Asher peeled his fingers away, one by one, slowly, delicately. "With the investigation and everything."

"Right. The investigation. I look forward to it."

The chandelier reverted into its original form as a lamp. The long skirt of my dress faded. And yet still, we were a princess and a prince in a castle.

"I like this version of you." I sat back into the chair, picking Asher's notebook off the seat, wondering how much of this was really him; he'd been so different at the party. "You should wear it more often."

I flipped to the last page of his notebook, which sat on my lap. A quote was scrawled on the parchment.

When devils will the blackest sins put on
They do suggest at first with heavenly shows
As I do now.

—*Othello.* 2.3.260-262

"Give me that." Force danced around his words. He lunged to take the notebook.

"The back isn't relevant. The suspects are only in the first half of the book."

He grabbed the notebook from my lap as if it concealed all his secrets. "I was about to give it back. No need to be so—"

"Sorry." Asher smiled. "I jot down my favorite Shakespeare quotes in the back, that's all. It's a bit embarrassing." A sudden wall built over his brown eyes, and I couldn't help but wonder what lurked behind it.

VII

*The voice of parents is the voice of gods, for to their
children they are heaven's lieutenants.*
—Shakespeare, *Double Falsehood: Third Series*

"MY DEAR BEXLEY!" Mom sang into the
phone. Hearing her soft voice was so refresh-
ing, so comforting. "I was gonna call you, but Drew said
I should give you space."

I snickered. "Oh, Mom, you should know you never
have to give me space."

"That's what I thought. Drew told me you'd want to
spend time with your new friends, not on the phone with
your annoying mother." Even through the phone, I could
tell she was making the face that she always did when
mocking my brother. "In any case, I'm so very happy that
you called."

I reminisced about simpler times, when I didn't need
to worry about clearing my name as a suspect for murder,
when my biggest worry was dreading schoolwork. Now

all that was a bygone fantasy. "Mom, do you know?" I asked nervously.

"Yes."

"I would think so. Did the Academy reach out?"

"They sent an email to all the parents. My heart breaks for that poor girl, Camilla, and her family. Did you know her?" The window above my bed provided a view of the stunning outside greenery, showered with sun. It was the third day of classes, and I was free during second period while Venus had class; I was alone.

Visions of the party came to mind—Camilla and my short yet sweet conversation. If she wasn't gone, I could've certainly seen myself growing close to her. "No." The less Mom knew, the better.

"I just feel so terrible. You went there to escape what happened with Abigail, and now it's happening all over again. Do you feel unsafe there?" she asked. "Please, tell me if you do because if so, I can bring you home."

"What about tuition? Would they give you a refund?" I blurted.

Mom hesitated. "Don't even worry about that."

No. Mom and Dad had saved up for so long to send me here. "Of course I feel safe. The police are all over Camilla's murder."

I'd been so close with my mother before the Academy. I'd told her vignettes from my days and confided in her. She knew everything from gossip to boys to my innermost feelings. But I couldn't tell her about my involvement in the investigation; she'd worry an unhealthy amount. "The teachers are amazing, really. And the campus is unbelievably stunning. You'd love it here, Mom."

"Promise?"

"On my life." It was the first time I'd ever lied to her on a large scale, and I felt sick to my stomach. "How are you? And Dad? And Drew?"

"Oh, you remember last year. Drew's been preparing like crazy for his standardized tests." She paused. "Well, you certainly didn't need to study as much as he does. Remember when you scored so well on your first try that they suspected you used dishonest methods?"

Of course I remembered. Rumors at Vista spread like wildfire: Bexley Windsor, the girl who cheated on her tests. "That was . . . funny." And certainly not the worst of the rumors.

"Are you enjoying yourself? Forming friendships? More than . . . friendships?" she teased.

"*Mom!*" I chuckled. "My roommate and I have really bonded, yeah. In regard to your last question, there is this boy. . . We might just be friends, though we danced together last night."

"You *danced* together? Is that a code word for something I shouldn't know?"

"No code words. We simply danced." I brushed the palm of my hand, remembering the soft touch of his. The night seemed like a dream every time I thought back to it. "It was amazing."

"Wow, these Grant boys are a different breed."

"I guess." I glanced over at my agenda, lying open atop my comforter. An array of unchecked boxes stared back at me, paired with assignments for each subject. "I'd better get going, Mom. I have tons of homework to get done."

"Of course," Mom said. "I'm glad you're enjoying the Academy, Bex. Love you."

"Love you."

A beep marked the end of our phone call. I hated being the one to hang up on her; I always made Mom do it. It'd become something like an unspoken inside joke.

Exhaling, I opened my math binder to the thick packet Bates had given us at the end of our first class. He wanted us to read the calculus notes to page twenty.

My phone buzzed, probably a text from Mom.

Asher

This meme reminded me about what we were talking about lol the Medusa thing.

Attached was a meme of a teacher asking a question to a class with a picture of Medusa's head pasted over it. Below was a student's internal dialogue: "Must avoid eye contact." I started typing back, trying to think up a witty response.

Why is that me when Mr. Bates asks me a question in calc hehehe

Asher

U have Mr. Bates? Oof. Pray for u.

He seems like a nice dude. Little creepy though.

Asher

Would u like some bloody crumpets?

Bloody crumpets? Ew.

Asher

Imao no I was being Mr. Bates.
His weird British accent

Never mind

OH HAHA. I thought you meant like the
crumpets themselves were bloody. Also
Mr. Bates's accent is hardly noticeable. And
nobody says bloody crumpets.

Asher

Bloody=British word, Crumpets=British,
therefore Bloody Crumpets=British.

Whatever u say. What even
is a crumpet?

Asher

Couldn't tell ya. R u free right
now or in class?

Freeee. What about u?

Asher

Same

My phone rang, and my soul very well might have left
my body. *Incoming video chat from Asher.* My hair sat tied in a
messy bun—not the cute kind—and I wore a sheet mask
on my face. I let my hair down, removed the mask, and
quickly applied some mascara. Somehow I still managed
to pick up on the seventh ring.

Asher wore an orange hoodie and grinned when I picked up. "I've been staring at the screen like an idiot," he said in a British accent.

"My dearest apologies," I reciprocated the lilt. "Whatever is your purpose for phoning me at this hour?"

His smile got bigger, which I hadn't known was possible. "Do I need a purpose, or could I simply wish to speak?"

"Of course, you may wish to speak."

"Very well. How has your day been?"

He wants to know about my day?

"It's been quite all right, all things considered. Though it's only just begun."

"Happy to hear such lovely news. I've slept in thus far, as my first two periods are free. How lucky is that?"

"Quite." I laughed, accidentally snorting. "Please pardon my ugly laugh."

"Nothing about that was ugly, Miss Windsor."

The butterflies again. "How kind, Sir McCoy. As much as I'd love to continue conversing with thy, I must attend to my duties. Duties equal calculus homework. After all, class does commence in approximately twenty minutes."

"Oh, no!" Asher said, exaggerating the accent even more. "I am not quite sure that was the correct usage of *thy*, but somehow you've pulled it off."

"Bye, bye." I bit my lip and hung up with a fluffy feeling in my stomach.

I was only up to page seventeen when the period-ending bell tolled. Cursing under my breath, I skimmed over the last three pages, absorbing as much information as I could from the text, before shoving my blue binder into my bag and leaving. Hopefully we wouldn't be tested today.

Studying the map from Mr. Trist, I figured out how to get to Mr. Bates's classroom. Racing through the campus, I didn't take in anything or anyone around me; I didn't want to be late the first week of school, which I was currently bordering on.

All the desks except for two were already filled when I entered the classroom. The bell that commenced class rang sharply barely a moment after my entrance. Relief washed over me.

"Lock the door behind you," Mr. Bates said, his lilt coming through as he spoke firmly. He looked almost too young to be a teacher, his smooth skin and mannerisms childlike.

"But there's one more empty desk."

"Lock it," he replied curtly.

Shutting the door, I made for a desk in the back corner of the room and exhaled. As I did so, a student knocked.

"I got it," I offered; I was already standing.

"No." Mr. Bates scrolled through his computer as he sat by his desk.

"No?" I asked, unsure if I had heard him.

"I was being nice for our first class. Students must be punctual." He projected the notes pages that I'd read last period onto the whiteboard. "Even you were cutting it close, young lady."

"Yes, sir." I glanced at the window in the door again; the student interlocked his fingers as if begging for mercy. Mr. Bates must've heard the repetitive knocks, though he seemed not to listen.

The class progressed at a painfully slow pace. Around

halfway through, the student disappeared from behind the window; he couldn't stay and linger forever.

I'll never be late to this class.

Math had never been my favorite subject. That's not to say I didn't excel at it—I'd been among the top students in my class at Vista—I just didn't find it interesting. I didn't get that rush of excitement from solving a math problem that I did from finding great meaning in a piece of literature or a work of art. Here, where everyone was an excellent student, I wasn't sure I'd stand out as much. If anything, I'd stand out in the opposite way; today, all I'd learned from Mr. Bates was how slow fifty minutes could seem. My math understanding hadn't increased in the slightest.

Mr. Bates said his last words of calculus and let out a grand exhale. "If any of you find you aren't understanding the material so far or haven't been comprehending the homework, feel free to stay after."

There was nothing I wanted to do less. But I thought about how much Mom and Dad had done for my education; I couldn't let it go to waste. Besides, next period was lunch, so I wouldn't miss much.

As the rest of the students poured out into the halls and the bells screeched, I remained at my desk.

"Mr. Bates, could I stay?" My stomach lurched for some reason.

"Of course. Here, take one of these other desks for now," he said, gesturing to a spot in the front row. "I can barely see you squeezed in that horrid back corner."

I dragged my book bag along the floor and took the middle front seat, right across from him.

"Do you have any specific questions, or are you just

having overall troubles?" His elbow on his desk, Mr. Bates rested his chin in his palm. "It must be really hard, being new this year, with Camilla and everything."

"You knew Camilla?"

"Ah, yes, she was a star student last year." Quickly, he pulled open his laptop, his back to the whiteboard on which he was projecting his screen. "Anyway, let me know what's troubling you, and we can talk about it. I can give you some extra practice, too, if you'd like."

I thought back to the notes. What *was* specifically troubling me? I barely even knew the material enough to answer such a question.

"All that stuff about limits . . . I mean, I was in a bit of a rush when I read it, so I'll reread it."

"Oh, yes. The language in that packet that I distributed seems to be rather convoluted. You know what?" He clicked onto his files. He didn't seem to realize that his screen was still projecting behind him. I didn't think it necessary to tell him. "I have another resource that might help explain limits through examples instead of all those incoherent words. I don't want calculus to make being new any harder for you. Though I can't seem to find the document in my files . . ." His brow knit in concentration as he continued to search his files.

"That's all right. I can find things online and reread the notes."

He shook his head, tapping his loafered foot steadily on the ground. "I know that I've sent this to students in the past. Let me look at my email."

He pulled up mail on his computer and scrolled down. "Limits packet, limits packet . . . ," he murmured.

My stomach turned when I saw Camilla Harding's

name, with the subject to the email as *meeting*. I didn't catch the date before it scrolled off screen, but it couldn't have been too long ago; he'd only scrolled for a few seconds before it appeared. It had to be recent, perhaps from over the summer. Only, why would they have met over the summer? Or maybe Mr. Bates didn't use his email frequently, and the message was from the end of last year or something. But everyone used their email; that couldn't be the case.

"Ah, here it is." Mr. Bates finally stopped scrolling when he found an email titled *Extra Help: Limits Packet*. "Let me send this your way, Miss Windsor. Do you have your school email yet?"

"Um, yes, thank you."

He raised his eyebrows, awaiting my response.

"Oh, right." Calculus suddenly seemed unimportant now. "That would be bwindsor@grantacademyforthegifted.students.com. I'll read that before next class."

"I'm sure you will." Mr. Bates grinned. "I'm always here for help if you need it."

"Thank you." I swung my bag over both shoulders as I stood. "I appreciate that."

Just as I made for the door, Mr. Bates's phone rang.

"Uh, yes, she's here," he said into the speaker after a moment. Mr. Bates gestured me to stay. "Yep, I'll send her down." He placed down the phone. "Your presence is requested in the headmistress's office."

"Why?" Every possible reason I could get in trouble sprinted through my mind.

"They didn't tell me, just asked to please send you down." He cocked his head toward the doorway. "Go on."

"All right, thanks, Mr. Bates." I pulled out the map from Mr. Trist. "I just have to find her office."

"Ah, it's close by." Mr. Bates jogged to meet me at the door. "I've got a few spare minutes before my next class—I don't mind showing you."

"Thank you." Though it was the last thing I wanted.

The walk was silent, thank goodness, while my mind was the opposite. Limitless questions filled my head— literally, they had nothing to do with calculus limits. More like, why was I called to the office? Was I in trouble? Was this about school?

About Camilla?

Headmistress Tuffin's office was modest in size and furnished with a velvet settee and an elaborate chandelier. On the far wall, dark green curtains parted to show two long rectangular windows with a view of the GAFTG courtyard. I'd only ever seen her from a distance; seeing Tuffin up close revealed more of the headmistress and made her appear more vulnerable.

"Hello, Miss Windsor!" she exclaimed. "I don't believe we've formally met. I'm Headmistress Tuffin, as you know. Welcome to the flock of Gifted Golden Eagles." Her voice was warm, welcoming, despite the two detectives who sat on the sofa to her right. She seemed to speak as if they weren't there.

"Thank you." I eyed the two officers, blood rushing from my head. *This is definitely about Camilla.*

"Of course. And hello, Mr. Bates. I assume you showed her the way?"

"Indeed." He waved and then disappeared from the room.

"Shall we address the elephant in the room?" Headmistress Tuffin glanced to the officers, then to me. "They just arrived and requested to meet with you. They'll be staying at the school for a little while, until the investigation is closed."

"Yes," the female officer spoke up. "We can take it from here, Mrs. Tuffin."

"I do believe you mean *Headmistress* Tuffin," she politely corrected.

"Apologies." The officer stood, the other following. "I'm Detective Morales. We'd like to bring her into the interrogation room, which we've set up on the other side of campus. Is that all right with you?" she said, turning her gaze toward me.

Interrogation. I'd hated that word ever since Abigail.

"I don't know that it is, honestly." Tuffin crossed her arms. I grew more and more fond of this woman with each word that she uttered. "She's already missing lunch for this, and she has class next."

"With all due respect, Headmistress, we have the right to question her." Detective Morales adjusted her blue uniform, strands of jet-black hair falling from her bun. She was an attractive woman, tall and with sharp features.

"Fine. Then do it here. The classroom beside this one should be empty now."

The two detectives exchanged glances, weighing their nonexistent options.

"That should suffice."

The tension nearly willed me to snicker until I realized what was about to happen. Then nothing seemed funny.

"Bexley, I must ask, are you okay with this?"

I nodded in response to Tuffin, knowing I had no choice.

"Come with us. It will only be a few minutes, and then you can resume your classes."

"What do you want to know?" I asked, trying to keep my fear at bay and hide the tremble in my voice.

"You're the closest thing we have to a witness." I followed them into the empty room and closed the door. If I wanted to, I could've involved my parents, but there was no use in disappointing them after all they'd done for me. For now, I'd just do as the officers said. The air smelled like a thousand rolls of tape. An oval table—similar to the one in Mr. Trist's room—filled the space. Crossing my arms over my chest, I sat opposite the two officers.

"I told the campus police everything I know on the night of the party. Didn't they pass that information on to you guys?"

"We'll need you to recount the exact events of the night of Camilla Harding's murder. We need to hear a firsthand account." Both officers took notepads from their bags and laid them on the table. "We'll also need to know where you were and what you were doing for the duration of the night."

"Fine." It would be better to put out the fuse before the fire ignited. Thoughts of a courtroom setting with an expensive lawyer defending me came to mind. "I didn't even want to go. My roommate, Venus, dragged me across campus to Beecher House."

"At which girls aren't allowed," Morales said as her assistant took notes.

"Yes, girls aren't allowed at boys' residences." I blinked,

hoping that doing so would make this all disappear. When I opened my eyes, the two officers unfortunately remained before me. "I didn't know the rules—I had just arrived at the Academy. I was just tagging along with my new friend, trying to fit in."

I struggled to keep my composure, wanting to yell. Sweat formed under my arms. But respect was my only hope at getting them on my side—that, and the truth.

"In any case, there are more important things. Whenever you're ready, Bexley, start talking," Morales said.

I ran through the events of the night, beginning at my arrival. Part of me felt uncomfortable sharing the whole closet dare with two strangers. Still, I gave every detail they asked for, down to the color of Asher's puke. "So while I was showering, Camilla laid out Asher's clothes on the bed for me to wear. I came back to that room after I was done, which was only, like, five minutes later. I thought Camilla was asleep, so I shook her to wake her up. Then I turned her over and saw blood dripping down her body." I saw her vacant eyes, her parted lips, as if I were discovering her lifeless body all over again. "Asher let me borrow his clothes, thankfully, so I—"

"I thought you said that Camilla laid out the clothes," Morales interrupted with an accusatory tone.

"Well, yes, she did. I just meant that Asher was fine with—"

"Which one is it?" Her voice was impatient now.

"I just said, I—"

"Your story has holes, Bexley." Morales jotted words down on her notepad. "We've interviewed most of Camilla's friends at this point. Everyone seems to have different explanations of what happened at the party. We want to believe you, but you're not giving us a seamless account of the incident."

"What do you mean?" I fought the urge to raise my voice. It was as if every word from my lips was under scrutiny. Closely evaluated, twisted and turned. "Camilla laid out the clothes while I was in the shower, and when I got out, I screamed at the sight of her, so many students fled. Venus was there, though, and Asher, because it was his room, and I think the boys that live there were probably downstairs. Asher tossed the clothes over to me and told me I could wear them." I wanted to add, *Why don't you interrogate them!*, but throwing my friends under the bus would do no help.

"See, you just changed it again." The officers seemed amused. "We're not saying you did it. We're only saying that with all of the plot holes in your story, we can't be sure that you didn't either. You can stay here to study at the Academy, but this investigation is far from over."

Beneath the table, I rubbed my finger over the scar on my knuckles, remembering. "I don't even have a motive. I mean, why in the world would I want to murder a girl as sweet as Camilla Harding?"

"Jealousy, revenge, utter loathing . . . I can think of plenty." The detectives stuffed their materials into their backpacks.

"Besides," said the stout orange-faced male officer who had hardly spoken thus far, "some people are sheer psychopaths."

"Like I said, I had no motive. I'd met her that evening and had known her for all of fifteen minutes. And during the time of . . . you know . . . I was in the shower." My throat began to strain.

Morales quirked a brow. "There are no cameras in there. What do *we* know? You could have left the water on in the bathroom and . . . and with everything that happened with Abigail Delaney, we can't be sure of anything," Morales said.

A chill seized my spine at the mention of her name.

How do they know about Abigail?

VIII

*And poise the cause in justice's equal scales, whose
beam stands sure, whose rightful cause prevails.*
—Shakespeare, *Henry VI*

PICKING AT THE oval table in English class, I
thought about what the officers had said.

This investigation is far from over.

They thought it was me; they had nothing to prove
otherwise.

"Are you all right there, Miss Windsor?" Mr. Trist's
visage came into focus before me. We were a minute or so
into class, and I hadn't absorbed a word of information.
I had to remember why I'd come to the Academy in the
first place: to get a rigorous education.

"Fine, thank you."

Jessie snickered from her seat; I forced myself not to
glance in her direction. A few chairs away from me, Asher
sat, clad in khakis and a polo shirt. He mouthed something to me, but I couldn't make it out.

"Today, we're going to talk about one of my favorite

literary elements." Mr. Trist seemed like the type of teacher who tried to appeal to teenagers. Students trickled in late. Unlike Mr. Bates had, Mr. Trist welcomed them. "Zeugma."

"The dance thingy?" Jessie asked, stretching her green chewing gum with her fingers.

"Please dispose of your gum. And I believe you're thinking of Zumba." Mr. Trist plastered a forced smile on his face, clearly seething beneath it.

"Gum? I'm not chewing on anything," Jessie said. She widened her mouth as one would at the dentist. "See?"

She swallowed it.

"Very well." His eye roll was not quite discreet enough. "Does anyone have a definition of the literary element for me?"

A hand shot upward. "A figure of speech in which a single word is used with two or more others in the sentence, usually in two different senses," the student said, their eyes glued to the computer screen.

"How original. You sound just like the dictionary," he said. "But yes, that is correct."

Another hand reached upward. Mr. Trist said, "I'm gonna ask you to hold your hand and your tongue." He seemingly couldn't resist laughter. "Did you guys see what I did there?" he managed between spurts of giggles. "I used zeug—you know what, no. Explaining the joke makes it less funny."

The class remained silent.

"No reactions? All right. Tough crowd." He hesitated. "Anyway, I'm going to ask each of you to come up with an example for me, okay? Bexley, why don't you start us off?"

"Um, sure." I wasn't good on the spot. What word could have different meanings? "The man lost his coat . . . and his temper."

"Not too shabby! The reason that worked was because she first used a literal noun and followed it with an abstract noun. Good." He nodded, impressed. "Drishti?"

"Uh, I don't know. Are we just supposed to come up with them on the spot right now?"

"I understand it's a challenge," Mr. Trist said. "Does someone else want to demonstrate?"

"Yeah," Jessie called out. "Bexley took a shot and Camilla's life at the party," she said, her eyes cold, willing me to refute what she'd just said.

"*Jessie!*" My stomach lurched, my dislike for her reanimated. She was ruthless. "That isn't funny."

"No, I don't think so either." She pursed her lips, crossing her arms over her argyle sweater-vest.

Classmates gasped. Asher and I made eye contact, shaking our heads.

"Can we just imagine that one . . . never happened?" Mr. Trist eyed me with . . . suspicion? I couldn't quite tell. "Bexley and Jessie, you two will stay after class. Jerome, all you."

The student nodded. "The farmer plowed his field and his—"

"Let's stop before you go where I think you will. That's enough zeugma for today! Jeez, I want to be your fun teacher, but I can't if you guys are acting like four-year-olds. I will say, though, those *were* all effective examples. I'll give you that much. We're gonna move on to rhyme schemes and observe some famous examples, including . . ." He continued to speak, yet his voice trailed off to me. All I could think about was how I needed to find Camilla's murderer before the whole school and the police officially accused me. My mind went to the email on Mr. Bates's computer. If she'd been his student last year, maybe they had simply remained in contact. Maybe he was going to write her a college recommendation letter or something.

After class ended, Jessie and I lingered to speak with Mr. Trist. He cleared his throat once the class emptied, changing his tone from playful to stern. "This is English class," he said. "If you two have something going on outside of here, leave it at the classroom door and pick it up on your way out."

"I'm sorry." Ironic how I was the one apologizing while she'd started it.

"Don't be sorry. Be better," he admonished.

Jessie ran her fingers through her russet locks. "It was the first zeugma example that came to mind, that's all. It was all in good fun."

My hands turned to claws, difficult to restrain.

"I don't want to keep you. You can go to your next classes." Mr. Trist ushered us to the door. Thank goodness Jessie and I were going in opposite directions for our next periods.

I heaved a sigh. I'd done nothing to make myself Jessie's target. Why me?

I held up the flash card to Eric, reading PO_4^{3-}.

"Phosphate!" Eric exclaimed, his green eyes lighting up.

"You're prepared," I said, thankful I didn't have to take chemistry this year. "You know all of these polyatomic ions forward and backward."

"Okay, good. Thanks for quizzing me." Eric smiled. Even though he'd appeared short-tempered when Venus and I had asked about Camilla, the guy didn't seem all that bad. Plus, I liked that he was giving me a chance, unlike most of the school.

"Any time."

I'd just told Venus of my dancing date—or not date—with Asher, as well as his desire to investigate with us—of which she approved—before he and some friends joined us. Asher, Eric, Venus, and I were seated at the table, along with one other student, whose name I hadn't caught, but now it seemed too late to ask. A nearby staff member hushed us, and we held back our laughs. We sat at a rectangular table in the library; it was our post-dinner leisure period. Though it was my second time in the room today, the striking chandeliers and high ceilings didn't fail to amaze me. Outside the long windows, stars illuminated the night sky.

"Ms. Petscher?" Venus asked, looking up from her notes. "For chem?"

Eric nodded. "Do you have her also?"

"Yep. I have that quiz tomorrow, too."

As Eric opened his mouth to respond, a staff member clapped their hands loudly two times.

"They do that to get attention here," Venus whispered to me, probably in response to my puzzled expression.

"All right, everyone." The library staff member stood in the middle of the room. "That concludes your free time. Please report back to your residences."

I gazed at the clock's small hand, which ticked to ten o'clock. Somehow, I wasn't even slightly tired despite the late hour. We said our goodbyes to everyone at the table, and Venus and I made our way to the exit of the library that led to the girls' dorms.

Asher jogged to catch up with us, though it was the opposite direction of Copley House, his new residence.

"Ash, come on, let's go back."

"I'll meet you there, Eric." Asher tapped me on the shoulder, leaving the spot tingling from his touch. "I can't believe Jessie would say that in English class."

"I can't believe it either." My heart warmed; Asher had gone out of his way—literally—to talk to me.

"What did she say?" Venus asked.

I glanced at the library staff member, who gazed at us with lethal eyes and crossed arms. "I'll tell you back in our room. Oh, and guys," I began, "I saw something this morning in Mr. Bates's classroom."

Asher offered a quizzical look. "Mr. Bates's?"

"Yeah. I saw this email from Camilla. I couldn't catch the date, but it seemed to be recent." I paused, trying to find the words to describe my apprehension of him. "Since the day that he first led me to my dorm, something seemed *off* about that man."

Venus, in a soft voice, said, "Midnight."

"Pardon?"

"Tonight, at midnight, we'll break into his room," Venus clarified.

"Are you crazy?" Asher's eyes widened. "Ever since the night of the party, they've been so strict about that stuff."

"Fine, don't come." Venus looked at me. "Bexley?"

I pursed my lips. "I . . . I don't know." *I'm already in enough trouble as it is, what with the police not believing my alibi.*

"Come on, we're not gonna find out essential information for the case if we don't bend the rules here and there." She squeezed my hand. "We'll go at midnight."

"You have your chemistry quiz tomorrow morning. Don't you need to study, get a good night's sleep?" I asked, silently praying she'd come to her senses.

Venus waved her hands in the air. "I'm prepared. It's a you-know-it-or-you-don't type of thing."

"Students!" the staff member shouted from behind me, making me flinch. How long had we been standing here? "It's time for you to say good night."

We parted ways. I turned my head over my shoulder to wave at Asher, but his back was already turned away.

"Please, please, please. Bexley, come on," Venus begged on the way back to our dorm.

"Fine." It wasn't out of my true judgment as much as it was out of pure desperation to halt her pestering pleas.

After we chatted for a few minutes upon our arrival back in our dorm, Venus crawled into bed and dozed off.

"What are you doing? Don't you want to stay up until midnight to go?"

"I still want my sleep." Venus rubbed her eyes. "I set an alarm for a bit before twelve—I'll wake up then."

"Whatever you say."

I envied Venus for her ability to drift into a peaceful slumber in mere minutes; insomnia kept me awake for hours some nights. Instead of trying to sleep, I pulled my sketchbook out from my bedside drawer. Venus liked to sleep with a bit of light, so I was still able to see my drawings.

Before I knew it, a rough charcoal sketch sat on my lap. The drawing illustrated a boy with parted curly waves and a conflicted smile: Asher.

I hadn't even intended to draw him.

Embarrassed, I closed the sketchbook as Venus's alarm screeched. It was a quarter to twelve. I hadn't noticed the time. Venus yawned and stretched out of bed. Her fatigue seemed to disappear when she stood. I didn't know how she did it. One minute she was sound asleep, the next chipper and ready to take on the world.

"Ready to do this?" Venus asked, tying her black curls into a ponytail, dressed in the same outfit as earlier.

"Not even a little," I said earnestly.

"Do you think your little *boyfriend* will end up coming?" She laughed.

"I assume he won't. And he's *not* my boyfriend." I bit my lip. *Not yet, anyway.*

"Whatever."

We hid blankets under our comforters and shaped them to mimic two sleeping girls. Just in case. Venus opened the door delicately. It seemed the softer she tried to open it, the louder the wood creaked.

We tiptoed out of the girls' dorm building, making sure the head of the dorm was asleep on our way—Venus pressed her ear to her door and promised she heard snores. Reluctantly, I scurried outside behind her. The midnight sky felt forbidden, and campus was the emptiest I'd ever seen it. Venus's phone flashlight illuminated a narrow path before us.

The only sounds our light footsteps, we entered Witz Building.

The darkness reminded me of Camilla's murder for some reason, which got me thinking. A little bit ago, Venus had mentioned a sound alibi.

"Venus?" I whispered.

"Yeah?"

"Remember when you were telling me about your alibi from the party? You never said what it was." I hoped my words didn't come off as suspicious.

"Yeah, um . . ." She didn't look at me. "That was kind of on purpose."

My heart stopped. "What are you saying?"

"No, no, don't worry. It's just—I want to tell you. I've *been* wanting to tell you. I really have. But I made a promise. She made me swear that I wouldn't tell anyone. We both told the cops, of course—"

"Who? Told what to the cops?"

"Pinky promise this stays between us?"

I nodded eagerly and hooked my pinky around hers.

"And after I tell you, let's not bring it up again." She moved her eyes to mine, and I could see in them an internal struggle. She let out a deep breath, and then the words spilled out of her. "Jessie. She's my alibi. She made a move on me, and I let it happen. We were outside, getting some fresh air. Things escalated. It was right after you and Asher went in that closet. She was pissed off, jealous, I think. Wanted to experiment. To not simply be the girl that pines after Asher McCoy. And I thought she despised me, but all of a sudden her lips were on mine and . . . and it was fun. Only happened that once, though. She was having fun, too. It was obvious. I just—I don't think she liked how much she liked it, if that makes sense. I couldn't care less who knew about it. But she made me promise to keep my lips sealed, pretend it never happened. So please, don't tell anyone. It would just complicate things. Not even Asher."

I nodded, trying to absorb what she'd just told me. *Jessie?* The same Jessie that Venus had never said a kind word about? A part of it made sense—how Venus was nowhere to be found after the closet ordeal, how Jessie hated me. Maybe her hatred was because she was jealous of all the time I spent with Venus. "Wow. I—Of course I won't tell. I'm sorry she wants to keep it a secret. That must be hard."

"Yeah. It's whatever."

All of a sudden, a silhouette appeared in the distance, sauntering through the darkness. "Venus!" I whisper-yelled. "There's someone here."

"Is that you guys?" I let out a sigh of relief; the voice belonged to Asher. "Venus and Bexley?"

"You came." A smile played across my lips.

In the darkness, I felt Asher approach, towering over me. "I caved. It was a good excuse to see . . . Mr. Bates's room." His words warmed the chilly night air.

"Come on, the classroom is right there." I pointed to the familiar doorway and immediately remembered the late student from this morning—yesterday morning, rather; it was now past midnight.

Venus pulled on the doorknob. "Locked." Not surprising.

"How were we planning on getting in here?" I asked, tapping my foot to an aggressive rhythm.

Venus kept pulling on the knob, as if doing so would magically unlock the door. "Good question."

"I got you." Asher rummaged through his pockets and pulled out a piece of wire.

I laughed, questioning why he happened to have that with him.

"What? I came prepared." A boyish grin spread across his face.

"No, nothing. Go ahead," I said.

"I just have a weird habit." He stuck the wire into the keyhole of the knob. "Unwinding paperclips is a nice stress reliever."

The wire fit perfectly into the hole, and the door opened on Asher's first try. Relief washed over me. "Let's go."

We entered Mr. Bates's empty classroom to find everything arranged identically to how it had been during class today. A perfect arrangement of desks—four by five—sat symmetrically before Mr. Bates's larger one. His leathery cologne still blanketed the dark air.

"What are we even looking for?" I scratched the back of my neck.

"His computer? His files?" Asher suggested. "I don't know, this was your guys' idea."

"Guys, we've gotta be quiet if we don't wanna get caught." Venus opened each of the desk drawers. "His computer isn't here."

"Of course it's not," Asher said. "Who would leave their computer sitting out at night? Mr. Bates probably brought it with him for the night."

"Great." I took a deep breath. "So we came here for nothing?"

"Relax, Bex." Venus angled her phone flashlight at each drawer she opened. "Look, his grade books."

Asher observed every corner of the room, as if answers would reside in the piles of dust. "Okay, and why would his grade books be of any help?"

"Better than nothing." I made for Venus's side. "Let's see if we can find Camilla. Here, let me take one. Asher, your help?"

Each book was for a different class section, shadows of the night casting over them. "Do either of you know which one she was in?" I asked.

"Nah. I didn't have Bates last year." Asher scanned the names that filled up the rows of the grade book he held. "Here she is."

His eyes looked drowsy under the phone flashlight.

"You don't seem very enthusiastic," I observed.

Asher shrugged. "I mean, we already know she was his student last year, so obviously she'd be in one of the grade books. I don't see how that will give us anything groundbreaking."

I peeked over his shoulder, tracing Camilla's row with my index finger.

Unit 1 Test 63%. Unit 2 Test 81%. Unit 3 Test 79%. Unit 4 Test 68%. Unit 5 Test 64%

More and more low test scores filled up the boxes following her name. "Maybe Camilla wasn't so perfect after all," I said, my jaw agape.

"But look." Asher pointed to the rightmost box. "Final grade, A-plus."

"That just doesn't add up—or average up." Venus shook her head, snapping a picture of the grades. "Do you remember what Chase told us?" she said, turning to face me.

I thought back to Venus's and my discussion with Chase. He'd said she was perfect, almost too perfect.

Especially in math.

Unless she wasn't.

At once, footsteps sounded from the corridor, nearing us.

"Bloody crumpets," Asher whispered violently—not the best thing to say when making me laugh wasn't the intention. "We're gonna get caught."

"Don't say that." Venus began shutting the drawers she'd previously opened.

"'Ello?" The man had a thick Cockney accent, muffled from the door. "Anyone 'ere?"

Asher placed a finger over his mouth. "*Security guard,*" he mouthed.

The guard hummed an unrecognizable tune, and his steps became louder. "Come out wherever you are." The security guard let out a deep breath that reverberated even through the door. We crouched beneath the large desk at the front of the room, squeezing each another's hands.

Please don't come in. Please don't come in.

The door screeched as he opened it. Each of the guard's heavy steps made my stomach lurch. He peered beneath each little desk. The guard's silhouette glided through the room for what felt like hours. Each step was one closer to us. What would happen if we got caught? The worst possible scenario came to mind: expulsion.

"A'ight then." He sauntered off, his sounds diminishing.

I let out a relieved breath.

"Close one," Asher whispered, closing the grade book. "Let's get out of here."

"Chill, he wasn't even close to discovering us." Venus wiped the dust from the floor off her bum. "We'll need to follow up with this, to get more evidence than mere grades."

"Agreed. For now, though, let's get some sleep," Asher said, stifling a yawn. I extended my arm to help him up and relished in the feeling of his fingers on mine. "Good night, Bex."

Bex.

"Good night."

Asher's hand lingered on mine for long enough to notice. He tucked a blond flyaway strand behind my ear.

"Ooh," Venus squealed.

In the darkness, I couldn't make out his face, but I knew he was smiling.

IX

There are more things in heaven and earth, Horatio,
Than are dreamt of in your philosophy.
—Shakespeare, *Hamlet*

SITTING CRISSCROSSED, I read over the limits packet from Mr. Bates. With each word, all I thought about was the man who had sent it to me. What had gone on between him and Camilla?

The dappled sunlight kissed my skin through the cherry blossom trees. I sat on my jean jacket while Asher rolled to lie with his back on the bare grass. Watching him hum along to music, I couldn't help but giggle. He closed his eyes, and I began to wonder if he felt the same way I did about us. People could be so hard to read.

"Did the police question you, too?" I asked.

He nodded, and I let out a breath of relief. Maybe I wasn't their only target.

"How was it?"

"Okay, I think. They just wanted to know my relationship with her, how long we'd known each other, all that."

"And what did you tell them?"

"The truth. Here." Asher extended his arm, offering one of his earphones to me. "Listen with me?"

I stuck the wireless earbud in my right ear, wondering why he hadn't mentioned anything of his alibi or other details. The triplet beats sounded familiar. "'Waltz of the Flowers?'" My voice must have been loud, trying to override the music in my ears. Thankfully, not many students surrounded us.

"You remember?"

"How could I not?" I said, a smile playing across my lips. "Don't you have schoolwork to do?"

He lowered the volume on his phone. "Probably." Yet he continued to lie down.

I guess I could read the calculus notes later. Lifting my hair up and spreading it around me, I lay beside him. Here wasn't the place to dance, but I had to admit that staring into his mysterious brown eyes was equally as enjoyable.

"Everyone here makes it look so easy." I thought about math, English, history . . . There was so much I had to do. "And then here I am, struggling to stay afloat." I sighed.

Asher chuckled. "Trust me, everybody's faking it."

"You really think so?"

"I know so." He picked out blades of grass. "The reason they make it look easy is because, chances are, they're not doing the work."

"Seriously?"

He nodded, tying the pieces of grass together at their ends. "Look, I made a bracelet." He tied the first and last blades together around my wrist.

"You're so multitalented!" I joked.

"Hey, my favorite lovebirds." I looked up to find Venus hovering over me.

Removing my hand from Asher's, I flinched. "Oh, hey there."

"Sorry to interrupt." Venus dropped her bag on the ground. "I have an idea. Do y'all mind if I join, or should I leave you two alone?"

"Don't be silly!" I patted the grass beside me. "Sit."

"Thanks, Bex."

The bell rang, signaling the end of the period.

"Oh, shit." Asher clambered to his feet. "I've got Euro history now. I'll see you guys later."

"Wait," Venus said. "I have to tell you the plan."

"The plan?"

"It's perfect." Venus rubbed her hands together. "You have math last period, Bexley, right?"

"How did you—" I began.

"You leave a copy of your schedule by your bedside, duh," Venus said.

"Fair enough." I listened intently, wondering what she'd make me do this time.

"I'll pull the fire alarm toward the end of the period, okay? So Mr. Bates will bring the class outside, and you'll stay inside. That way, you have at least ten minutes to investigate his computer."

I cringed just thinking about what would happen if I was caught. The first time I'd let Venus cajole me into something, it hadn't gone so well. "I don't know about that."

"Please. I would do it if I had Mr. Bates. Unfortunately, you're the only one of us who does."

I weighed the pros and cons. Yes, getting caught would

suck, but not nearly as much as being arrested would—
and not nearly as painful as being ridiculed by the entire
grade had been. Or at least what felt like the entire grade.

Asher tapped Venus's back, which presently faced
him. "And what's my part in this?"

Venus wagged her finger. "You stay quiet. Don't tell
anyone about this little scheme. If it's possible, start a rumor that there was a little fire in some room."

"Okay." He waved his goodbye and flashed his infa-
mous dimpled smile, then started on his feet. He and I
both knew he wasn't about to start a rumor.

"Do you have class now?" Venus asked, fiddling with
her backpack strap.

I shook my head. "Two frees in a row."

"Nice, nice."

I skimmed one example on the packet from Mr. Bates
before getting bored. Out of my growing curiosity, I
wanted to ask Venus more questions about her alibi—
where outside she and Jessie were, how long they were
there for—but I had to respect that she'd said she didn't
want to talk about it anymore. Instead, I went with, "It's
so great that Asher's so passionate about finding Camilla's
killer."

"Yeah." Venus plucked piles of grass from the ground.
"I can't say I'm surprised, though. I mean, the two were
certainly close."

"Close?"

"Oh, I don't actually really know. Anyway, what did
you say you had next?"

"Asher never told me that. Why would he keep that
a secret?" I continued, ignoring her attempt at trying to
change the subject.

"Told you what? They were close, that's all. It probably just wasn't relevant." She shrugged coyly. "Besides, Camilla has been *something* with most of the grade. Even she and *I* were briefly a thing, though it ended up evolving into a friendship . . . mostly." Venus appeared to be in deep thought at the mention of this, staring off into the distance.

It seemed more and more dimensions of Camilla kept unfolding.

Suddenly I thought back to the party, when Camilla had mentioned Asher not minding if she sat in his room. Why would that be? Had they been more than just friends?

Venus was right. Asher had no obligation to tell me. *Right?*

I stared at my calculus notes, annotated with colorful erasable pens. The alarm should sound any minute now; I had to figure out a way to stay behind. If I remained idly by my desk, Mr. Bates would obviously make me come with the class outside. Sweat lined my spine, my stomach somersaulting at the thought of what I was about to do.

I raised my hand. "May I use the bathroom?"

"You don't need to ask," Mr. Bates said flatly.

I managed a half smile and escaped into the hallway in search of the nearest bathroom. Hopefully, the alarm would ring soon; only a few minutes were left of the period.

Halfway down the hallway was an empty restroom. I locked myself in a stall—which was probably an unnecessary step—and waited. Scrolling through my phone to pass the time, I hoped I wasn't missing too much in calculus. The grass bracelet Asher had made fell off my wrist and onto the dusty bathroom floor.

A notification from Asher popped up on the top of my screen: *Good luck on the stunt* 😃. I got that stirring feeling in my heart that had become frequent the past few days.

And then, *beep-beep, beep-beep.* The shrill of the fire alarm made me flinch. I had to be quick; I had no idea how long Grant fire drills lasted.

Once the noises in the corridors mellowed, I unlocked the bathroom stall and splashed water on my face. "You can do this," I told the girl in the mirror.

Though everyone was outside, I still felt the need to tiptoe as I entered Mr. Bates's room. Thankfully, his computer sat open on his desk, unlocked from him using it right up to when the alarm had gone off. A sticker sat to the side of his touchpad, the bottom left curling up. It was a golden eagle, Grant's mascot.

The keys felt forbidden on my fingers. I opened his mail and searched *Camilla Harding* in the search bar. The meeting email I'd seen earlier popped up on the top, with a long string of replies following it. The messages weren't from her school email.

From: Camilla Harding <camichic@buzzmail.com>

To: David Bates <dbates@grantacademyforthegifted.com>

David, I can't let this continue. I'm telling the police everything unless you make it happen. Why haven't you been responding to my texts? You know that I have the power to put you behind bars.

From: David Bates <dbates@grantacademyforthegifted.com>

To: Camilla Harding <camichic@buzzmail.com>

Camilla, why are you doing this? You don't mean it. Was this your intention the whole time? To manipulate me?

An onslaught of questions filled my mind. I took out my phone and snapped pictures of the emails to show Venus and Asher, and maybe others if it came to that. Tremors of unease surging through me, I pulled up his texts and searched for Camilla's contact again. Next to it was a smiley emoji. A long chain of messages appeared. I kept scrolling up, but the texts never ended. I stopped scrolling when I got to a certain point: February of last school year.

Camilla
Hey, thanks for the "help" lol.

> Any time. You know you can come here whenever you have trouble 😉

I scrolled down to the more recent ones, my hands shaking.

Camilla
Stop doing this.

Fucking answer.

I don't have as much control over the elite system as you think. I'm doing everything I can.

Camilla

What you did was illegal.
We both know it.

You were the one who started this all. Are you serious, Cam?

Camilla

Don't call me that.

I'll tell your fucking wife.

Make me an elite.
You're on the board.

Or I won't hesitate to tell the cops everything you did.

What do you mean "everything I did"? I didn't do anything.

Camilla

Do u really think your feelings were reciprocated?

Yes! You started this.

Camilla

And I'm ending it, too.

For the record, I hated our time together

You only did it so I'd give you good grades and make you an elite, didn't you?

You didn't know that I don't have the power.

Camilla

Make me an elite. Or I'm telling the cops.

I'm trying the best I can.

Camilla

Do u promise you'll do it?

I've given you an A+ for my class and suggested you to the board. That's all I can do. You'll probably get the spot if you're good in all your other classes. But no, I can't promise. I don't have that damn control.

Sleep w/ Tuffin if u want the spot so bad.

Camilla

Haha. I guess I'll tell the police then.

You can't do that.

Camilla, you can't.

Camilla

Watch me do it. You'll lose your job and your wife. And your freedom.

I won't let you do that.

Camilla

What are you gonna do to stop it? Huh?

That was the last message. Received August 27.
Three days before Camilla's death.

Indistinct chatter began to sound from the hallway, so I frantically snapped pictures of the texts and exited the messages, careful to cover my tracks. Before students and teachers got too close, I scurried into the bathroom. Through the small window in the brown door, I watched lines of students file back into their classrooms, my heart hammering in my throat.

My hands trembled as I grasped my phone and viewed the texts again in disbelief. Was I reading them right?

After waiting a few moments in the restroom, I crept back into Mr. Bates's classroom. Exhaling, I was relieved the plan had gone so seamlessly.

"Bexley Windsor!" Mr. Bates called as I returned to the classroom. "Where were you during the fire drill?"

After reading his texts with Camilla, I saw the ugly lies twisted beneath his eyes. The man was filthy and deceitful. All I could picture was him plunging a knife into Camilla's chest.

"I'm so sorry. I couldn't find you guys outside, so I wandered around campus looking for you." I crossed my fingers behind my back, hoping he'd believe me. I hardly felt bad lying to the man after all he'd done.

"You're lucky that it was a false alarm and you're not a scorched piece of bacon." Mr. Bates shook his head. "Next time, you're gonna have to stick with our class. We'll be right outside this building, okay?"

I nodded, swallowing down the confrontation that begged to spill out of my mouth. "Okay."

As Mr. Bates opened his mouth to resume teaching, Tuffin's voice on the loudspeaker bellowed through my ears. "Attention, students and faculty of Grant Academy for the Gifted."

Mr. Bates pointed to his ears, encouraging the students to listen carefully.

"Please lock the doors and remain in your classrooms until you hear otherwise." Tuffin paused for a moment. With a shaky voice, she added, "A student has been . . . Er, um, there has been a terrible accident."

X

It is not in the stars to hold our destiny but in ourselves.
—Shakespeare, *Julius Caesar*

FOR THREE HOURS, we sat locked in a classroom with a liar. A predator. By the end of it, the ends of my fingernails were completely bitten off.

Finally, the loudspeaker screeched to release us from this prison at eight o'clock. When the headmistress began to speak, all the students listened intently, hoping for more information. "Students and faculty of Grant Academy for the Gifted," Tuffin began, "we have searched every room and corridor. Nobody is lurking in the Academy. You are all safe and free to return to your dorms. Police are on-site and will remain here for the next few days. Even with them here, we suggest you travel in groups as an extra precaution. Our grief counselors are equipped to help you. More news will come in the following hours. I know this is incredibly hard, but we'll get through it. We're Grant Academy for the Gifted. Lastly, we'll be adding a sign-out system to the Academy to ensure our students' safety. We sincerely hope it won't have to come to shutting down GAFTG. Thank you."

Finally, we could leave. The students rushed out of Mr. Bates's classroom, some of their cheeks wet with tears. Mine were stiff and cold—curious.

What happened?

My eyes transfixed on the ground, I pondered the possibilities.

Is someone else dead?

For centuries, there had been complete safety at the Academy. And then, suddenly, GAFTG becomes the center of crime? I believed in events occurring by chance, but not like this. This was no coincidence.

I'd been so deep in thought that I hadn't noticed Asher coming up in front of me. "Bexley!"

"Oh, thank goodness." I placed a trembling hand on his shoulder.

"I need to tell you something. Come on." Many anxious students filled the halls. He nodded toward an empty offshoot of the corridor. Grabbing my hand, he guided me there.

"What the hell happened? Do you know?" I asked. We were alone now.

Asher held his phone with shaky fingers. "Eric. Eric Fernsby."

My jaw dropped.

Eric Fernsby.

"What about him?" But I was afraid I already knew the answer.

"He didn't deserve to die." Asher sniffled. "I wish I'd

taken advantage of our friendship before it was wiped away."

"How do you know what happened already? I'm so sorry. I can't imagine." In fact, I didn't need to imagine. I could just *remember*. Last year at the lakehouse.

"Suzuki texted me a long-ass paragraph, like, a minute ago."

I embraced Asher in a hug, my head resting on his shoulder. It was obvious he needed it. "How does he know?"

"He was in the headmistress's office already. Apparently Suzuki was in trouble because he'd been talking back to his teachers or something. That part's irrelevant." He lifted his head so that his face hovered over me. "Tuffin and her assistant were talking about it right in front of him, as if they forgot he was there."

"Oh my goodness."

"I know." Asher shook his head. "Chase said that the body was found looking different than Camilla's. Some kid found him lying on the floor of the boys' bathroom, bloody all over. Officers are in there now, investigating. Instead of being stabbed in the chest, it looked as if Eric was murdered without a weapon, by a person's literal hands. Battered to death."

I pictured the scene and cringed. Why did misfortune have to follow me wherever I went? "Does that mean it was a different person than Camilla's killer?"

"It could be. Or it could be the same person using a different method."

Is this going to be a pattern? Is someone else going to be next?

"This is all so crazy." I'd hardly known Eric. Still, his death shattered my heart into more pieces than it had already been split into for Camilla—literally, my chest ached. I could only imagine the pain that those close to him and Camilla had to endure. Their poor families. "Who would do such a thing?" My voice cracked.

"Think about it. Nobody else knew about the fire drill besides me, you, and Venus."

"Okay, and . . . ?" I didn't like where this was going.

"Venus knew you would be inside, surfing Mr. Bates's computer. She knew you'd be the only one who was absent at the fire drill. She knew you'd be easy to—"

"Frame?" I stared stone-faced at Asher.

"Exactly. You were the only one who wasn't outside. And she won't tell me her alibi. When Camilla was murdered, she could've been anywhere." But how could he know I was the only one inside during the fire drill? And what were *his* alibis for both murders? I shook the notion.

"No way." I wanted so badly to tell him Venus's alibi, but I'd made a promise, and I'd keep it. "She didn't do it. She would never murder someone—ever. Call me adamant. Call me stubborn. It's not her fault that our plan misfired."

"Okay, Miss Adamant and Stubborn, it's the only thing that makes sense right now." Asher stared deep into my eyes with a longing gaze, begging me to accept the possibility.

I wouldn't. Venus was my one loyal friend. "Do they even know for sure that the murder took place during the fire drill?"

He pulled up the text from Chase on his phone. "Could've been before or during fire scare, they don't know yet," he read aloud. "But probs during it—that would make more sense."

The loudspeaker beeped. "Students to their residences. I repeat, students to their residences." There was urgency in the speaker's voice.

"We should go back." I pulled out of our embrace. "Venus didn't do it. And trust is the cornerstone of any relationship."

"Fine."

"Fine what? Fine, you trust her?"

"I mean, I can't be sure of anything." Asher pressed his lips into a thin line.

"Just say that you trust her," I pleaded.

"I can say it, doesn't mean—"

"Please, Asher. She wouldn't."

"Okay." He exhaled. "I believe you." But his hesitant gaze contradicted his words.

"Good. And anyway, she was outside during the drill and in class before it," I said. *But* was *she outside?*

"Yeah." He began to walk away. "I hope prank week doesn't go too crazy."

"Prank week?"

"Oh, right. Sometimes I forget that you're new. The grade is split into two teams, and for a week, we pull all sorts of pranks on each other. It's always the second week of school—well, first Friday to the second Friday—best week ever." He pursed his lips. It felt wrong to hear him talk about something as normal as prank week in the present circumstances. "With Camilla and Eric gone, I wonder how it will play out."

"I'm surprised they're allowing it to happen this year. Seems kind of insensitive."

Asher placed a finger over his lips. "They're not. They never do. It's student tradition."

"What are the teams?"

"They're up in the dorms. You haven't seen? You and Venus are together and with me." He played with his light brown curls. "It's a shame—Suzuki is on the other team, and he always wins. Anyway, see ya."

Asher was already well on his way back to Copley House when I remembered the whole purpose of the fire stunt. I'd been so distracted by what he had to say about Eric that I'd forgotten to show him the photos of Mr. Bates's messages with Camilla. Oh well. I'd have to show him at dinner; it wasn't something to reveal over text.

Gentle brushstrokes of pink and purple glided across the sky outside the window. I sat in a booth beside Venus, who wore a purple blouse, and Asher sat opposite us. The dining hall was magical this time of day, grandiose architecture looming over us. Students seemed like walking zombies with numb eyes. A constant hum of chatter hung in the air.

Asher and Venus hovered over my phone screen, their jaws agape at the text messages. "'What are you gonna do to stop it, huh?'" Venus read the last message aloud.

"Shh."

"Remember what I told you the day you arrived here, Bex? That guy's a fucking creep." Venus winced. "I knew there was something suspicious about him, but *this*? I never would've thought."

"So he and Camilla were . . ." Asher grimaced, unable to bring himself to say the words. His eyes were bloodshot; I wished I could numb his pain. He had to lose Camilla *and* Eric. "They had . . ."

"An inappropriate relationship, no question." Venus blinked at her Bolognese pasta, unable to stomach her meal after gleaning the new information.

"What should we do about it?" I asked.

As if it were obvious, Venus said, "You gotta tell the cops."

Contrary to our last encounter, I was strangely looking forward to talking to the detectives. Though we didn't know the exact details, we had enough to make Bates look guilty.

Is he?

The question lingered in my mind. My evidence made him look suspicious. That didn't mean he was definitely Camilla's murderer. However, right now he was the best we had. Once I showed everything to the officers, he'd be in major trouble. And my name would be cleared . . . I hoped.

Even if he wasn't the culprit—which he did seem to be—he'd had an incredibly weird relationship with Camilla, which had to be illegal.

The night was dark, past sundown. Because of the three hours we were locked in Mr. Bates's room, the day felt as if it had gone on for years.

I knocked on the door of Tuffin's office, and she quickly opened it. The lighting was dim, and her face was drained of color. "Hi, Headmistress Tuffin."

"Dear, you're supposed to be in you dormitory."

"I know, but . . ." *I believe Mr. Bates murdered Camilla Harding and quite possibly Eric as well.* "This information is vital to the Camilla Harding investigation."

"Is that right?" She shut her computer screen. "Shall I put you in touch with the officers?"

I gulped down my hesitation and nodded. I could've reported the messages immediately after the fire drill, but I'd wanted to show them to Venus and Asher first.

"All right." She took the vintage glossy black telephone and dialed. "Let me phone them." She soon put the phone down and said kindly, "They're on their way."

Within a few minutes of awkward silence and tapping my toes, the same two officers from yesterday arrived. "Oh, it's you again," Morales said, her tone strident. "Headmistress, do we have to stay here again? Or can we take her to the interrogation room?"

"The classroom you used last time should be available." Tuffin gestured to the doorway. "And Bexley, please go straight back to your dorm after this."

"Of course. Thank you, Headmistress." I smiled politely.

We went to that same adjacent room. I walked sandwiched between them, feeling the heat of Morales's eyes on my back.

As we arranged chairs and sat down, Morales looked tired, not only in a sleepy sort of way. She wore a white blouse and a navy suit, which appeared to have been thrown on at the last minute. "So, do you have a reason for summoning us at quarter after ten, or did you just want to mess with us?"

"No, I have something important to show you." I unlocked my phone and pressed on the photo app, trying to steady my hands, hoping they wouldn't ask how the information was obtained; the fire drill stunt we'd pulled would most definitely land me in trouble.

"Going on your phone?" Morales crossed her arms. "And by the way, is there a reason you weren't present at the fire drill?" she added, catching me off guard.

A chill descended my spine. How did they know about that? Perhaps I should tell them what we'd done; it would give me an alibi for the drill. Still, none of that would matter once Mr. Bates took the blame. A thought nagged at me—why would Bates kill Eric, too? Or was it somebody else?

"I told Mr. Bates—I was there, but I couldn't find our class. Being new, it's still hard to get around. If you'd allow me, I'd like to explain the purpose of this urgent meeting." Before they could continue on the topic of the fire drill, I pulled up the photos of the text messages and placed the phone on the table, swiveling it to face them. "Mr. Bates and Camilla were engaging in . . . clandestine meetings."

"'Xcuse me? Miss Harding and Mr. Bates? The elite board member and math department head, Mr. Bates?" Detective Morales said incredulously.

They must have done a lot of investigating already to know that much about the Academy staff. "That's the only Mr. Bates I know."

The officers exchanged curious glances. "And how do we know this isn't a load of crap? He was at the fire drill, while you weren't."

I pointed to the phone. "See for yourselves."

I tried to push down the hesitation within me, but a question kept bubbling back to the surface: Mr. Bates was outside during the incident. Could he have done it before? Or had someone else been working on his side?

The rotund male officer whispered the texts aloud, his eyes bulging from their sockets. "Wait a minute. Couldn't you have edited this? These days, you can easily text a friend and then change their contact name."

Shrugging, I said, "I suppose that's possible. If you don't believe me, take him in yourself and question the man."

Morales's tone became serious. "Send us these photos, please. Now."

"Will do." I emailed the photos to the address she provided.

"And how did you obtain these? Did you hack into his computer or something?" *Here we go.*

"No, I—" I should've thought up an excuse before coming. "He let me stay after class to look at a math packet on his computer. He ran to the bathroom and told me I could pull it up when he was gone. I didn't hack into anything. The messages popped up right away when I was trying to find the packet." I calmed my nerves about lying, reassuring myself that once the officer obtained the evidence, they wouldn't care that I had falsified how I got the messages.

Morales eyed me suspiciously but remained silent. I took it as a win. "These messages could give him probable cause. We'll bring this guy in for questioning," she mumbled to the other officer. "You're free to go, Bexley."

I exhaled my worries and headed for the door, sweat soaking through the underarms of my shirt. Mr. Bates would finally get what he deserved.

"And hey, thank you," said the male officer. It was the first ounce of respect they'd given me.

"You're welcome," I said, turning to leave.

I shut the door, and a grin crept across my face. News would spread fast in the Academy. Perhaps students and the police alike would finally believe that I wasn't responsible for Camilla's tragic fate.

XI

Suspicion always haunts the guilty mind.
—Shakespeare, *King Henry VI*

IN THE DAYS following Eric's death, memorial services and police interviews replaced classes. It was as if someone took a knob of Grant Academy students' enthusiasm and turned it so that it was just above silence. Darkness hovered over everything we said and did. Students were scared to leave their dorms after Eric's death was revealed. But today, we were finally back in class, and getting back into some order felt good.

The substitute teacher for Mr. Bates had a knack for teaching that the head of the math department himself lacked. He had dimples and a long black ponytail. "All right, that's all I have for you guys today. Let me know if you have any questions for me."

A student raised his hand. "What happened to Mr. Bates, and when will he be back?"

I'd anticipated the whole grade to learn about the Mr.

Bates scandal, but it wasn't spreading as quickly as I'd thought. Hopefully within a few days it would become common knowledge. That would finally shift the blame off me.

"He's um . . . not feeling well," the substitute teacher said. "Anything else? No?"

The bell screeched. Next was Shakespearean Literature, the worst class because I had to see Jessie, yet the best class because I could see Asher. The thought of him sent butterflies fluttering around in my stomach.

Though it was only the end of the first week, I was beginning to learn how to navigate the vast Academy. Rain teemed down on me, continuing unabated for the entire duration of my walk to Mr. Trist's classroom. I splashed in puddles as I jogged, wishing I had an umbrella. My clothes were soaked through. Morales appeared in my peripheral vision with an umbrella, walking a bit in front of me. I kept my head down, hoping she didn't notice me. We'd left off on a good note, and the last thing I needed was to be interrogated again, or worse, accused. Thankfully, she didn't call my name.

Squeezing water out of my soaking hair, I entered English a few moments before the bell. My mind overflowing with thoughts, I didn't observe my surroundings enough to catch what awaited below my seat. I didn't even consider why today I had a swivel chair when it had always been a wooden one. As I settled into the chair, Jessie stared at me, seemingly holding back laughter. And when I sat, I understood why.

A terrible noise blasted through my ears, abruptly stopping when I stood.

What the heck?

I sat back down, and the loudness began again. The class laughed in unison, but Jessie's voice seemed the loudest. I felt around beneath my seat to find the air horn taped to the chair.

"And *that's* how you start prank week!" Jessie's long red hair draped over her shoulders. How was she spending her time on pranks after another student had *died?*

I stared at her in disbelief. My face felt hot as I attempted to unstick the horn from the chair.

"Sorry I'm late." Mr. Trist strode into class, sipping tea from a ceramic mug. "We just had a faculty meeting. To be honest, every day I lose a little bit more faith in humanity." He set his mug on his desk and opened up his laptop.

I assumed the faculty meeting was regarding Mr. Bates. Part of me was grateful for Mr. Trist's tardiness; he didn't have to witness my embarrassing prank.

Asher mouthed, *"It's okay,"* from across the room. And with that, all else seemed trivial.

We read a few Shakespearean sonnets, which reminded me of the back of Asher's journal. I couldn't resist looking over at him throughout the period and admiring the interest in his eyes.

Before I knew it, class was over, and I made for my history classroom, which was all the way across campus. Asher had to go the opposite direction, so I walked alongside bright green hedges in solitude. Thankfully, the rain had stopped. Leaves were beginning to turn red and orange in color. Autumn was upon us. I thought about the outfits I'd brought to the Academy; the majority of my attire was better fit for the warmer seasons. Oh well. I'd borrow some of Venus's clothing and make do.

"Bexley!"

I looked to my right to find Brandt Harding. He stalked toward me, tall, his black coat flapping in the breeze. I hadn't expected him to remember my name or to be on campus.

"Hey, what's up?" I asked, furrowing my brows. *Why would he want to speak to me?*

"I know this might come across as weird to you, but I've been in close contact with the officers investigating Camilla's case." He looked better; his face had more color. His sharp features and gelled hair reminded me of the outcast-turned-good-looking kid in every high school movie. "They've told me—quite irritated—that you're interested, too."

"Oh." I managed an awkward laugh. "I mean, I suppose."

Is he just hanging around on campus for the fun of it?

"I received this note." He plucked a crumpled sheet of paper from the pocket of his joggers. "You know a lot about this case. Does it mean anything to you?" he said, handing it to me.

THIS HALLOWEEN IS ABOUT TO BE EXTRA SPOOKY. IT'S YOUR TURN, BRANDT. IT WOULD BE RUDE TO TAKE ONE HARDING AND NOT THE OTHER. PREPARE YOURSELF FOR A HALLOWEEN NIGHT FULL OF BLOOD. AND NOT THE COSTUME KIND. DARE TO SHOW THIS TO THE POLICE, AND YOUR FATE WILL MEET YOU SOONER.

The threat was written in orange ink, nearly blinding. A shiver seized my spine. "Are you sure it's not part of prank week?"

"I received it early this morning, in my hotel room. Everybody knows that prank week doesn't begin until first period." Brandt shook his head. "Besides, I don't even attend Grant anymore."

But . . . Mr. Bates.

He'd been gone since dinner last night—taken into custody, I'd assumed. From then on, I hadn't a clue what they did to him. Nonetheless, it didn't add up. If the note *was* from this morning, Mr. Bates couldn't have written it. And even if it was somehow written before then, why would Mr. Bates want to kill Brandt Harding? Come to think of it, what about Eric Fernsby? Bates had a connection to Camilla but not to Eric. Unless there was something I didn't know.

Unless Mr. Bates isn't the culprit.

"There's a huge Halloween blowout every year," Brandt said. "Every student attends, no matter their usual social life."

"I bet it won't happen this year." I snapped a photo of the note.

"Of course it will." Brandt folded the note back up. "You've got to come, Bexley. We can catch the murderer once and for all."

"To a party? No way. If the calamity on August 30 taught me one thing, it was to never go to parties." The memory replayed in my head: the closet, the blood, the screaming . . . "I'm sorry. I can't."

"Halloween is over a month away. It's only September."

Brandt put the note back in his pocket and made praying hands. "You'll think about it?"

"I'm not going to a party. And why should you? Why would you want to put yourself at risk? Besides, you're not even a student here anymore." *Just go home,* I wanted to say.

"I'll protect myself." He adjusted his glasses. "Don't you want to find Camilla's murderer?"

"Well, yes, but there are other ways." I resumed walking. "I'm sorry, I have Euro history class."

Brandt tugged on my backpack, forcing me to stop.

"Ow." His pushiness was almost crossing the line. Why had he sought me out alone, without Venus or Asher?

"Bexley, you *need* to go to this party. Please, heed my words. The murderer will be there. We'll take them down together," he said with eager eyes.

"I'll think about it."

Returning to my dorm after a long night, I felt refreshed after finally spending some time alone in the library. I had to keep my priorities straight. I'd come to the Academy for the pure purpose of education. I'd signed into the building upon my entrance and made the tenuous climb up the stairs that seemed to become easier each time.

Studying alone was always more productive than with a friend. Though I loved Venus, when we were together in the library, the conversation always shifted to conspiracies about the investigation. Tonight I'd finally knocked out my history reading and gained a true understanding of the calculus material.

Doing homework in solitude brought a certain serenity that I wasn't sure was common or unique to me; as I studied, I found myself forgetting about my other worries and focusing simply on the work. After all, my problems seemed frivolous in comparison to the French Revolution, about which we were currently reading in class.

Now I was ready for a peaceful slumber.

Opening the door, I expected to find Venus sitting on her bed, but the room was empty. She was probably with a friend. My heart strained at the realization that she had many of those, while I had only one: her. Well, her and Asher, though what he was to me remained a mystery. But right now, I had more important matters to worry about than popularity.

As I stepped into the room, I was assaulted with the overwhelming smell of air freshener. It wasn't merely a single spritz, no—the entire room was damp with liquid. My eyes stung, and sudden sneezes escaped me.

What the hell? Where is it coming from?

Lo and behold, the air freshener bottle sat on my nightstand, a zip tie tight around the trigger. I raced toward the can, shielding my face with my hands. As I felt my comforter, liquid pooled in my hands. I couldn't sleep on that. Across the room was Venus's bed, soaked in the exact same substance.

How long has this been spraying? And who would have the nerve to do this?

As if reading my mind, the can stopped just as I neared it with a scissor, ready to cut the zip tie. It seemed the bottle was completely emptied.

Screw prank week.

As soon as I pressed send, little circles appeared; he was already typing back.

Asher

LOL. What happened?

> Air freshener EVERYWHERE in our room. I have a pounding headache now.

Asher

Bloody crumpets. That sucks. What are you gonna do?

> idk. Def can't sleep in here. It's all over my comforter.

Asher

I mean . . . I have an idea.

> ?

I grinned down at my phone.

Asher

First of all, is Venus w/ you?

> No idea where she is.

Asher

If you have nowhere else to go, you can come over here . . .

Perhaps these prank week shenanigans weren't so terrible.

> Isn't that like strictly against the rules?

Asher
Shhh

I pondered the possibilities. Even simply sitting in this chemical-scented hell for another few minutes gave me a pounding headache, let alone attempting to sleep in here for nearly eight hours.

> Okay. I'll be there in 5.

Gathering pajamas and my toothbrush in a drawstring bag, I couldn't help but become giddy. I tiptoed, careful to avoid waking the head of the dorm. Making my way out of the dorm hallway and into the stark night, I felt like an illegal spy. It was only 10:25, but above it looked like midnight. Stars aligned in the calm but cool evening sky, forming beautiful constellations, reminding me that this universe was bigger than me. Thankfully, the campus was empty. Still, I felt wrong about this.

I remembered how to get to Copley House as I thought back to the party at Beecher House; the two buildings were fortunately side by side. Venus and I had walked there so oblivious. My largest concern on my way to the party had been the friends I'd make. *Not murder.* Of course not. How could I have known?

Asher lived in a giant house with all of his friends, almost like a college fraternity. That must be fun but a bit overwhelming, at least for me. I recalled filling out the housing form back in May. I had the option to live by my-self, with one roommate, or in a house. Grant Academy for the Gifted had to be one of the only high schools to give that sorority-like option of a house.

Save that for college, I recalled Mom saying.

Right. College. I had applied to a bunch of schools early, and now I was simply trying not to stress. I'd see early results in mid-December and the rest in March or April.

Looking back, I was happy with my choice to live with one roommate. At the time, though, I'd been leaning to-ward living alone.

Mom had taken my face in her hands and said, *You'll get lonely, darling.*

The house in which Asher and his friends resided was painted white with long columns stretching upward. I couldn't make out many details of the exterior in the blackness.

The moment I sent Asher a message letting him know I was here, he swung the door open. "You actually came," he said, eyes beaming. He wore an orange hoodie and black sweats.

"I told you I would." My eyes scanned the ground floor of the house as he welcomed me inside. When I'd been in Beecher House, strobe lights illuminated the room and bottles of liquor could be found in every area. Now, here at Copley, all that littered the ground were half-finished bags of snacks, which was somewhat comforting. A main room with a TV and gray couches was beside a kitchen with a marble countertop, stools around its perimeter.

"Yo, Bexley," Chase said. My gaze shifted to him, sit-ting on the couch with a video game controller in one hand, the other wrapped in a black sling. Beside him sat a friend that I was sure I'd seen around, though I didn't know his name. He had messy red hair and freckles, and he nodded in my direction while keeping his eyes on the TV.

"Oh no, Chase, what happened to your arm?"

"Intense arm wrestle." He flashed a grin. The arm wrestler opponent must have been incredibly aggressive to leave him like that. "What are you doing here, anyway?"

"Hey," Asher said, "be nice. Someone pulled an air freshener prank on her. Her whole room smells like a bath product store times one thousand."

"Oh, yeah, I remember Jessie telling me she was gonna pull that one on you and Venus." Chase put down the controller and chuckled. "Your team is totally going down."

Of course it was Jessie.

I wondered if she knew that I knew about her alibi on August 30. Part of me wanted to pull a prank back on her, but I had neither the time nor the immaturity for that. I would *not* stoop to her level.

Blood splattered on the television screen within the video game. Chase's friend threw the controller across the room. "Hey, bro, you made us die in the game."

"My bad."

"Want to go upstairs?" Asher asked me. "We have an extra room in here. You can sleep there."

"You're serious, bro?" Chase interjected, arms crossed, which looked difficult with his sling.

"Suzuki, I'm not gonna make her sleep on the floor. It sucks, but Eric's room is free."

Chase pursed his lips. "Eric's room isn't for guests. Besides, it's blocked off with tape."

"We'll figure something out," Asher said to me before quickly changing the topic. "Hey, Suzuki, where were you at breakfast this morning? I was planning on pulling an epic prank," he said, flashing a mischievous smile.

"I must have slept in. Can't say I was too bummed to miss it. But seriously, don't bring her into Eric's, okay?"

"Okay!" he retorted. Asher took my hand in his and led me upstairs. "For now, you can just chill in my room."

He creaked open the door to his room. "Sorry about my friends. They can be . . . interesting."

I sat on his blue comforter—a slightly lighter shade than the one he'd had in Beecher. The overall setup was similar to what I remembered of his old room. It smelled like boy—strong but pleasant cologne. "This is so against the rules."

"That makes it so much more fun." He patted the space beside where he lay, and I obliged. As I rested my head on his chest, I felt safe in his arms.

"There's something more serious that I should tell you."

"Serious? Do you mean serious or *serious*?"

"Serious, I don't know. Brandt Harding showed me some note that he received. It was written in neon orange ink, and it said he was 'next.' I don't remember the exact wording, but it said that he would die on Halloween."

Asher slapped his hand to his mouth. "Oh my goodness. On Halloween? I mean, that is in over a month. And what about Mr. Bates?"

"He got the note after Mr. Bates was already taken into custody by the police. It can't be from him." I shivered; a draft came in through the open window. "And to your point about Halloween, exactly. We need to figure it out before then." I shook my head. "Or else we'll have to go to the party on Halloween night."

"Why would we go to a party? After what happened with Camilla, I never want to—"

"I know. That's why we're going to find the culprit before October thirty-first. We'll save Brandt and whoever else they wanted to kill."

"At the rate we've been going? We can't find anything, Bexley."

"We'll have to." But I didn't sound very convincing as I said it.

"Bexley, you can't go to that party." I looked up to find a pleading look spread across Asher's face.

"Please don't coddle me."

Asher groaned and ruffled his hair. "Does that mean it's a different person than who killed Camilla?"

"That's the thing. The note said something about taking both Hardings. *Both* implies that it was the same person who murdered Camilla."

"Bexley, what have we gotten ourselves into?" Asher cracked his knuckles. "You gotta go tell the detectives that Bates didn't do it, then." Dread filled my chest at what he was suggesting.

"And make myself the primary suspect? No thank you. Besides, the note threatened that his 'fate' would come sooner if he showed the police."

There was a moment of tense silence.

"We both know it's the right thing to do," he said.

"I know." I sighed. "Mr. Bates is still a predator, though. He *should* be in jail for having a relationship with Camilla and abusing his power like that."

"Go in and tell the detectives what you know, then leave it in their hands to finish the investigation. Please?"

I sighed. "But imagine if I were to tell them and the note stayed true to its word. And Brandt would be . . ."

I looked into his eyes, silent.

"Can I at least see the texts again?" he asked.

Handing him the phone, I said, "They make him look so suspicious."

"They really do." He scrolled through the photos. "You're sure these are real?"

I took my head off his chest. "Of course they're real, Asher. What are you suggesting? You think I made this up?" I focused on containing the anger that started bubbling inside. *How dare he?*

"No, no. I trust you." He placed his palm on my cheek. "I trust you. But what if Eric's death isn't related? What if he was killed by someone else, or what if he . . . killed himself?"

"I mean . . . I haven't even thought of the possibility. Wouldn't we know, though?" I asked. "Wouldn't the police make that clear?"

"I don't know. They're not releasing much information. And . . . it's not like you can just look at someone and tell. Except—he didn't like to talk about his parents a lot, but when he did, he said that they often neglected him. And—oh gosh—we were so mean to him and always excused it by saying it was a joke. But there hasn't been a suicide at GAFTG since a double pact, like, ten years ago." His voice quavered.

"Whatever happened to Eric, it wasn't your fault. And would suicide even make sense with the way the body was found?"

"I have no clue. I mean, like I said, they don't seem to be releasing any information. I don't think so, though. The only stuff I know about the body is what I already told you. This whole situation just couldn't be any worse," said Asher. "As his friend, I should've noticed something was up with him. I mean, he had pretty bad anger issues. He'd lash out over the smallest inconveniences. And he was seeing the school counselor pretty consistently."

"You didn't do anything wrong. How could you have known?" I held his hand. "We don't have to talk about it."

"No, it's okay. I've been talking to the grief counselor, and it's . . . helped." Asher yawned and stretched. "Tired?"

I nodded. I'd been exhausted since the moment I left the library. "But I feel bad sleeping in Eric's room. Besides, that would be creepy."

"Not to mention, Suzuki would drag you out of there by your hair."

"I guess I'll have to stay here, then."

"Oof, that sucks." His sparkling eyes contradicted his words. "How unfortunate."

Those butterflies started up again, stirring about my stomach. "What do you guys do here on weekends?"

"Well, there are no classes, of course. We get to sleep in and do pretty much whatever we want. You'll see tomorrow." He gently brushed my flyaway hairs out of my face. "Before all of this, Friday and Saturday nights were epic. Now they'll be . . . interesting." Asher got up to shut the blinds before pulling up a playlist on his phone. "Here, 'Sleepy Classical.' It lulls me to sleep every time."

"Good night, Asher." We both got under the covers, and he rolled over so his back faced me. I thought over the conversation we'd just had, half wishing I was still in his arms instead of a foot away from him.

"Good night, Bex."

A few moments of classical music passed. I stared at the shadows on the ceiling.

"Do you ever get homesick here?" My voice sounded small.

"I . . . No, not really," he said. "I'm happy to get away from my mom." It came out in a joking tone, though there seemed to be a lot more there.

"Really? I'm sorry."

"No, no. Really, it's fine. She's just . . . Well, she sent me off to get rid of me. I guess I'm glad to get rid of her, too, so it's a compromise. Benefits both of us."

"I'm sure she loves you. People just show love differently."

"By tearing you down?" he asked, the humor gone.

I brushed my fingers over my scar as Abigail sprang to mind. That fatal October night. *Could you be any lamer?* She'd teased me out of love, right?

Asher continued, "Work out more. Your hair looks bad. You suck at piano. That outfit is ugly. Why don't you take up law, like me? My mom wants me to grow up and be exactly like her. Act this way and look this way and do this thing and—oh my goodness, I need to shut up."

"No, you don't." I reached out and gently touched his back.

The sheets rustled, and Asher turned to lie on his back. "I never talk about it with my friends. She wants the best for me, she really does. But my best is never enough." His voice began to break.

"It's okay, you can cry," I said.

"I don't cry."

"Okay, big man," I mocked. I found his hand in the darkness and took it in mine, his palm warm and comforting. "It is enough, though. I promise, okay? More than enough."

"Thanks. I mean, you really don't need to—"

"You know it's okay to talk about these things, right?"

He paused. "I'm talking about them with you right now."

"I mean with your friends. It's like you said that time—you wear two faces. It's like you're hiding from your friends."

He peeled his fingers away from my hold. "That two faces thing, it was a joke."

"Doesn't seem like one to me," I mumbled. It was quiet for a moment.

"Good night." His words were sour.

"Wait, why are you mad? Did I say something?"

He was either asleep or pretending to be.

"Sleep tight, I guess," I whispered.

The clock on his nightstand presented a red 11:11. I used to always make wishes if I was awake at that time.

I wish that my family will be happy and healthy. I wish that I'll get good grades this semester.

I shut my heavy eyes.

And lastly, I wish that the murderer of Camilla Harding and Eric Fernsby will rot in prison.

"Morning—or afternoon, I should say." I awoke to Asher hovering over me, shirtless and in flannel pajama bottoms, toothbrush in hand. "Seems like you slept well."

I looked to the clock. 12:04.

"Holy crap. I never sleep this late." I'd slept for over twelve hours. How was it past noon already?

"Don't sweat it." He walked to the blinds and rolled them up. "You were tired."

I stretched out of bed and realized I hadn't even changed into my pajamas last night. Jeans still fell stiff around my legs, and a T-shirt with smiley faces clung to my upper body.

"You want to take a quick rinse off?"

"No thanks." I thought back to the night of Camilla's murder. "I'm not planning on ever showering in a boys' house again."

At once, I remembered what Venus had said about Asher and Camilla's relationship. And what Camilla had said at the party: how Asher would've been okay with her hanging out in his room.

"Okay. You can leave, then," he said curtly.

"Wait, I—"

"I'll be downstairs. The boys are making lunch." He turned to leave the room, pulling the door shut behind him.

Was he actually mad at me about last night? The string of my bag was looped around Asher's standing lamp. I hadn't touched it since I'd arrived. Yawning, I glanced at myself in Asher's mirror in the front of the room and nearly gasped. He'd seen me with my hair a mess, breath reeking.

I took the comb that sat by his mirror and attempted to brush the knots out of my hair. After thirty seconds of futile combing, I gave up and tied my hair up in a bun, removing two pieces by the front to frame my face. The outfit I wore was the one I'd put on before the library, but the pajamas I had in my bag weren't much better.

Goose bumps formed on my forearms from the cold air, abnormal for a September morning. Shivering, I descended the stairs and made for the kitchen. The room was much too nice for a residence for teenage boys. The RA had his nose in a book on the couch. Plates sat piled in the middle of the marble countertop. As I entered, the boys halted their chatter and looked to me. Seven boys sat around a rectangular table, munching on sandwiches. They chewed with open mouths and licked condiments from their fingers.

One familiar boy with curly dark hair grimaced. "What is she doing here?" He didn't even attempt to whisper.

"Sorry, I'll go," I said, heat flushing my cheeks. I turned toward the door, looking over my shoulder at Asher. He dropped his half-eaten piece of bread and blinked back at me, not saying a word. Why was he acting so weird?

I let out a breath of relief as he stood and walked over to me, but each step seemed unsure. "It's freezing out," he whispered.

"Yo," Chase said. "Get a room, you two." The rest of the boys laughed at his remark, though their voices were dull. Clearly, Eric's death had taken a toll on the group. Chase seemed to be a leader of sorts. Within moments, they resumed their barbaric conversation.

"Wait here for a second."

"Here? With all of your friends?"

He was already halfway up the stairs. "Just for a second," he called back.

I stood awkwardly, trying not to attract attention. Soon, Asher returned with a gray sweatshirt in hand. "Take it." It dangled from his outstretched hand.

"Are you sure?"

He nodded. "Just give it back to me soon." He cocked his head toward the door. "Don't want you to freeze."

"Okay. Thanks." I forced a half smile as I took the sweatshirt from him.

Without another word, he closed the door behind him. What had I done wrong?

XII

There is nothing either good or bad, but thinking makes it so.
—Shakespeare, *Hamlet*

AS IT TURNED out, the weekend could pass extremely quickly when it was spent catching up on assignments and slumber and attending tennis tryouts. I'd never played before, but sports were required at Grant Academy. They'd been put on hold because of the murders but were now back up and running.

An empty canvas sat before me, waiting to be drawn on. All the others already had sketches, while I couldn't decide where to start. It'd taken me fifteen minutes to find this room. About a dozen students filled the benches around three rectangular white tables. Paintings decorated the walls, and the smell of acrylic paint wafted through the air. My charcoal pencil sat stiff in my hand. To my right and left, brushstrokes populated my periphery. However, in front of me was only blankness. A white, unmarked canvas.

The only vision that came to mind was the first thing I saw whenever I tried to dig into my memories: Camilla, slain atop Asher's navy comforter.

"Are you just gonna sit there and stare at it?" a girl with two dark braids asked, grinning. She'd introduced herself earlier as Eliza, leader of the art club. Now, during today's leisure time, I finally got around to attending. However, most club members already had nearly completed pieces.

I tapped my charcoal pencil steadily on the table. "I'm thinking," I said, trying to smooth the edge in my voice.

"If you need any help, feel free to ask." She smiled.

At least people were beginning to treat me like a normal human being; Mr. Bates had been arrested—if not for definite murder, for the affair—and finally the students knew I wasn't guilty. Some were even acting extra nice; they must have pitied me for being accused for so long.

Only four people—that I had knowledge of—knew Mr. Bates wasn't the true culprit: Asher, Venus, Brandt, and me. Asher, Venus, and I had discussed that it'd be better to find the villain before notifying the police of Mr. Bates's innocence. Brandt must have remained quiet as well—for his own reasons, perhaps. Whatever they were, it didn't matter; his silence worked in our favor.

But did Mr. Bates really have nothing to do with Camilla's murder?

He couldn't have. The same thoughts continued to spiral and spiral through my head. The text messages had to be an unlucky coincidence.

Without thinking much, I pressed the pencil to the canvas and began drawing something. What it was, I didn't yet know. Hopefully it would figure itself out. I wasn't used to working with canvases; my only previous work had been in my sketchbook, save for certain art assignments from Vista High.

I shouldn't have ever left.

Bad thoughts, Bexley. Bad thoughts.

There was nothing I could do; I had to make the most of this unfortunate situation.

The way Asher had given me his sweatshirt made me internally squeal, though it seemed he'd been doing it out of obligation. I thought about his perfect face, his sharp features, his . . .

Eyes.

That was what I'd been drawing, without even knowing it. The crescent shape touched edges with its inverted twin. Between the two was a pupil that hid many secrets. I flicked my pencil up from the eyelid in gentle strokes to form plentiful eyelashes.

"Pretty."

I flinched, turning my head. Eliza peeked over my shoulder, observing my process as if she were an apprentice watching a master. "You know, you're kind of a superstar."

"Thanks. I mean, it's just an eye, nothing too—"

"Not about that, silly." She grinned. "Though your eye is pretty cool, too. But I'm talking about what you did for Camilla. She finally has justice now. You made Mr. Bates pay for what he did. And everyone that once accused you feels terrible."

"Oh, thank you." A pang of guilt hit me, heat rising to my cheeks.

"Don't blush. It's a compliment, that's all," said Eliza.

"Thank you. I appreciate that."

Soon I'd get the real killer arrested, and I wouldn't have to feel contrite for wrongfully getting Mr. Bates in trouble. He may be a bad man, but he wasn't a murderer. It just didn't make sense with the timeline of events.

Eliza returned to her project, leaving me lonely in a room filled with chatter. Solitude hardly bothered me. Though I didn't take part in the conversation, I eavesdropped on the exchange that occurred on the other side of the table.

"Esteban hated him?" one girl said. They were already mid-conversation. "Tech wizard Esteban? I didn't know that."

"I'm just confused about Mr. Bates. I know he killed Camilla because of their secret . . . love affair. But why did he kill Eric?" *He didn't.* "Were they having an affair, too, or something?" the other girl said.

The first girl laughed. I must've missed the humor.

"Anyway," she continued, "Eric and Esteban used to be inseparable, remember? Then during sophomore year, Eric completely ditched him to hang out with Suzuki's group . . . the 'popular' kids. I'd hate him, too, if I were Esteban."

I alternated between looking at the girls and my canvas. "You know I'd never ditch you."

The other girl giggled. "Duh."

Esteban.

I'd need to talk to him.

Nobody even noticed that I left art club less than fifteen minutes after arriving. I left my canvas on the table and exited with my backpack swung over my shoulder after signing out. I jogged to the bench at the end of the empty and silent corridor before taking out my computer and pulling up the student directory.

Esteban. I typed his name in the search bar, hoping I'd spelled it right. The charcoal from my hand smudged on the touchpad of my laptop.

A portrait photo of a boy with a toothy smile appeared. *Esteban Navarro.*

I'd probably had seen him around; his face was familiar. All student emails were the same: first initial, last name, @grantacademyforthegifted.students.com. Quickly pressing my mail app, I addressed an email to enavarro@ grantacademyforthegifted.students.com. For the subject line, I typed: *Urgent.*

I wasn't quite sure where I was going with this, but I needed to find the murderer soon. Eric's ex–best friend could perhaps be a step in leading me there.

Hello Esteban,

Bexley Windsor here. I was wondering if you'd have a few free minutes to meet up with me and talk. Let me know ASAP.

Thanks,
Bexley

Three days slugged by, full of my impatient waiting for Esteban's response and more pranks. Thankfully, I wasn't the subject of any of them. The air horn and air freshener had been enough. Only one day remained of prank week.

I'd told Venus about the new lead, but she didn't seem too impressed for whatever reason.

In line for some flatbread for lunch in the dining hall, I found a boy in front of me, scrolling through his phone. From the back, his hair seemed to resemble Esteban Navarro's from the photo in the directory.

"Esteban?" I said, clearing my throat.

It would be awkward if it wasn't him. The boy directly in front of me whipped his head over his shoulder. He had a long, straight nose and olive skin. "Do I know you?" His voice was shaky and a bit awkward. "Wait a minute. You're Bexley, the girl who found Camilla and all that, aren't you?"

My one personality trait.

"That would be me, yes."

"Cool. Why'd you . . . say my name?" He looked confused.

We moved up in the line. "Have you seen your email lately?"

Esteban shrugged. "I don't check it much. Why?"

"Just wondering." I managed a polite smile, tucking a stray blond hair behind my ear. "Do you have a few free minutes to talk?"

The lunch lady slid a slice of flatbread onto his tray. The dish looked surprisingly appetizing: thinly sliced and topped with the perfect amount of sauce and vegetables.

"*You?* You want to talk to *me?*"

"What's wrong with that?"

His cheeks flushed. "I mean, sure. I guess I could talk." His voice was high-pitched, as if he was still going through puberty. "Do you have lunch now?"

I looked down at my tray, then back at him. It seemed self-evident to me. "Yep."

Esteban began walking toward a circular table in the corner of the dining hall. "What do you want to know?" he said, pulling out a chair to sit.

"I hear you were close friends with Eric." I followed his lead and pulled out the chair beside him.

"Eric." He scratched his forehead. "Key word—*was*. I hadn't talked to him at all this school year before his, um . . ."

"Right, right." I took a bite of the flatbread, the entire tomato slice gliding off with it. Though chewing, I wouldn't wait to swallow; information was imminent. Covering my mouth, I asked, "What was your relationship like after you two drifted apart?"

"Drifted? Where'd you get that word?" Esteban swallowed a messy munch of pizza, cheese dripping out the corners of his mouth. "He full on ditched me. That kid did me wrong. I probably shouldn't have said that—it makes me look suspicious, doesn't it?"

"No, not inherently."

"Okay, good." He played with the stringy cheese with his fingers. I fought against the urge to gag. "You know, you're not the only one to dabble in the investigation, Bexley."

"What do you mean?"

"I know a little about technology." He swallowed down his last bite of pizza and took his laptop out from his book bag. His voice now a whisper, he said, "Who do you think hacked the Academy system to find out our grades early last year?"

My eyebrows furrowed. I suddenly thought about

Mom, who loved playing around with computers. So much for calling her frequently.

"He's got two thumbs, and he ain't bad looking," said Esteban.

"I wonder."

"It's me. I'm the hacker." Esteban's thin lips curled into that same toothy grin from the student directory photograph. "Nobody can blame me—the staff really thinks it's best to wait until the end of the semester to show us our grades. All of the students thanked me immensely, plus the staff switched the system to showing us our grades month by month. Technology wizard. Navarro the nerd. I've heard 'em all." He pressed a few buttons. "I'm often underestimated."

"That's cool and all, but what does it have to do with the case?" I said impatiently.

Esteban beckoned me closer, and I slid my chair over to his side.

"This has nothing to do with me being best friends with Eric. In fact, it's not even about Eric. I couldn't find anything about his murder. It's about Camilla."

"What is?"

"I've hacked the school cameras and gathered all the footage I could find during the weeks of Camilla's and Eric's murders. But there aren't cameras in every room. Not in the bathroom in which Eric's dead body was found after the fire drill. Not in some hallways."

Esteban was right. This kid wasn't to be underestimated.

"Wouldn't the school already have reviewed the camera footage?"

He shrugged. "I'm sure they have. But I don't trust anyone but myself. So I decided to take the case into my own hands. The faculty is so secretive, and, you know, it happened twice. I'm doing what I can to stop it from happening a third time."

"Have you told anyone about this?"

"Nah. I need irrefutable evidence before going to the police." He pushed his tray to the middle of the table so he could replace it with his laptop. "Besides that, I don't have many people to tell. And like I said, I'm not very trusting—not since Eric backstabbed me, anyway." It seemed like this guy really hated Eric.

"Well, you can tell me."

Esteban arched a brow. "Why should I?"

"I . . . Well, what do you want?" Surely, as a hacker, he didn't need my help to obtain any secret information. "I'll do anything."

"There's not really . . . Well, actually, you any good at writing?"

I leaned forward in my seat. "I'd say so. Why?"

"I do have a paper for French history that I haven't gotten around to."

I jutted out my arm. "Done."

He shook my hand tentatively with a nod. "I'll send you the assignment. It's fifteen hundred words. You sure?"

That was kind of a lot of words. This had better be worth it. "Yep."

"This stays between us. You do look like someone who would keep a secret."

"Thanks?" I wasn't sure if that was a compliment or not.

He angled his laptop toward me and clicked on a file on his desktop. "This is the most relevant thing I could find. There was also a video of Camilla and Mr. Bates from a few days before the murder, fighting in his room. No microphone, so I couldn't hear what they said. You figured that one out on your own, though."

So Camilla and Bates were fighting in person after the texts?
"Yep."

"Anyway, in this clip, Camilla isn't too far away from where we're sitting right now." She and another girl were sitting in the dining hall. Camilla wore a purple sweater and had her hair tied in a bun. The dining hall was empty save for a few other students in seats that were distant enough to be out of earshot.

"Who is that?" I pointed to the dark-haired girl who sat across the table from Camilla in the footage. She looked somewhat familiar, probably from seeing her around.

"Rupi Khatri. She's a senior, Camilla's ex. You didn't know?"

I shook my head. It seemed I was learning new things every day. Things that everyone else already knew.

The time stamp in the bottom right corner said *3:07, August 30*.

The day of the party.

My blood froze in my veins. "That's from, like, less than six hours before the party."

"I know. Now look, Rupi's about to pick up her cup." Esteban spoke as if he'd watched the clip hundreds of times before, able to anticipate every movement. "Cup shatters in three, two—"

In the video, Rupi dropped her mug, which split into a million tiny fragments. Camilla covered her face with her hands. Her body began to shake, as if she was crying, though it was difficult to tell within the grainy footage. The clip ended with Rupi storming off, leaving Camilla at the table. Camilla banged her forehead on the table three times and put both middle fingers to the sky.

"Have you talked to Rupi?" I said after a few beats passed.

Esteban crossed his arms. "I don't talk to anyone."

"You're talking to me." I stacked my tray on top of his and took the last bit of crust in my hands—the best part.

"*You* approached *me*."

"Whatever. I'll talk to Rupi," I offered, wondering why he hadn't done anything about this yet.

"No!" He raised his voice for the first time. "I mean, please. Don't talk to Rupi. Or, at the very least, don't tell her I showed you this." He looked panic-stricken.

"All right. If it makes you feel better, I won't share my sources with her, Esteban."

Just then, his phone buzzed in his pocket. He pulled it out and exclaimed, "Sweet! I've been waiting for these."

"What happened?"

"My shipment of stuffed animal rats finally arrived. I was starting to think they would never come." He smirked. "I'd better go retrieve those. Bye, Bexley." He rose and started walking away.

"Rats?"

"Prank week," he called back over his shoulder, a sly grin on his face.

I waved goodbye, grabbing the stacked trays. I needed to tell Asher and Venus about this. Though the information from Esteban wasn't what I'd expected, it introduced a new potential suspect: Rupi Khatri.

XIII

Though this be madness, yet there is method in't.
—Shakespeare, *Hamlet*

THE DOOR WOULDN'T open. I'd come empty-handed—no unwound paperclip, no strategy. Why had I thought that breaking into the English office at midnight would do any good?

I'm officially going mad.

The picture of Brandt's note was pulled up on my phone, ready to match. In Mr. Trist's first class, he'd asked us to jot down answers to a few questions about ourselves. He'd said that all the seniors did them, and they'd remain in the English office until the end of the year, when we'd compare our answers from the beginning of the year to our answers at the end.

The question forms were all handwritten; a perfect way to identify who'd written the note to Brandt and if the murderer was, as suspected, a GAFTG senior.

Now, I stood before the door in the pitch-black

midnight corridor, tugging on the doorknob as if pulling harder would somehow open the locked door. *How stupid could I be?* I couldn't get in here without a key or at least something that worked as one. Coming here was so unlike me. But some of Esteban's words rang true to me. *I don't trust anyone but myself.* Ninety-nine percent of me trusted Asher and Venus, though how could I be sure?

What's gotten into me?

The past couple of days, I'd made no progress in the case. Rupi seemed to be impossible to get ahold of, and she was all I had right now. She hadn't responded to my emails, and I didn't have any classes with her.

Every time I thought about Mr. Bates, guilt froze me in place; he was being imprisoned as a murderer when he couldn't have been the culprit. Hence, I needed to find the actual killer. Then Mr. Bates would get fair treatment. I had to keep reminding myself that he was still a predator; it was the only thing that made me feel better, even if only the tiniest bit.

Though the night was freezing, beads of perspiration dripped from my forehead. Fists clenched, I pounded on the door, realizing moments later that it was a stupid idea.

Taking a deep breath, I turned around, back toward the dorm. Luckily, the English office wasn't too far from the girls' dormitories. An indoor route existed between the two, so I wouldn't have to traverse the campus alone in the middle of the night.

This investigation was supposed to get easier as time went on and more evidence was collected. But unfortunately, finding a murderer wasn't so easy, especially when they were skilled in their methods.

Saturday morning struck me like a bolt of lightning. The week had passed by incredibly quickly. I'd thought there was a lot of homework the first week of school, but the second week nearly doubled it; teachers began to pile assignments on us as if we were robots. And having to write Esteban's French history essay had proven itself more difficult than I'd anticipated. I researched tirelessly before even putting fingers to keyboard. Vista High was nothing compared to this. I'd complained about a singular assignment. When the Academy had mentioned "academic rigor," this wasn't what I'd expected. Oh well. I'd come here for an education, after all.

Sadly, the increasing workload left me no time to see Asher lately, not that he wanted to talk to me. A week had gone by since I'd slept over in his room.

I began typing a text to Asher.

> Hey, how has your week been?

Venus was sleeping in, and I didn't want to wake her. She looked so peaceful, her features soft in the dim light. I decided to go to the dining hall alone; my stomach desperately growled, begging to be fed. I dressed in plaid pants and a navy long sleeve and quickly brushed my hair, tiptoeing through the darkness of our room. I left a Post-it note on Venus's nightstand: *at breakfast if u wake up.*

Sauntering down the somewhat-filled hallway of the girls' dormitories, I scrolled through notifications on my screen, responding to memes from Drew and long-winded texts from Mom. At once, a sharp fist punched my shoulder.

Ouch.

I looked up to meet Jessie's eyes, cold and green. "Watch where you're going." She walked alone, clad in a polka-dotted nightgown.

"What did you do that for?"

"Do what for? You bumped into me." She offered a fake frown, mocking me. "You're lucky prank week is over, Bexley. Great ideas keep coming to me." She snickered as she walked away.

Is this really about Camilla anymore? Or does she just hate me?

The latter had to be true; Mr. Bates was largely thought to be the culprit, and she had no reason to think it was me anymore.

Unless she knows of Mr. Bates's innocence.

No. She couldn't.

Don't let her bother you. Become impervious to her remarks.

Muttering the same affirmations to myself hardly did anything; the mere sight of Jessie's face made me want to punch a wall. Still, I knew it was more likely her problem than something I'd done.

My phone buzzed.

Asher

It was all right.

Meet for breakfast @ dining hall?

Asher

ok

In a few minutes, Asher and I sat opposite each other in a booth in the bustling dining hall. The sun filtered through the windows, kissing my skin and leaving a shadow. We sat on green and gold cushions, which matched Academy colors. He pulled off a gray hoodie and a bedhead like nobody else could.

"I'm sorry. When I said that thing about the two faces, I—"

"It's okay. It's not your fault. It's just . . . I opened up to you, and then you acted just like her. Just like my mom. Had to criticize some part of me." He stared at a chip in the wood on the table.

"I didn't know you felt that way. I'm sorry. You know that wasn't my intention," I said quietly.

"Don't worry. Let's not talk about that. I've missed you." Reaching across the table, he cupped my face in his hands, smiling genuinely.

The words made me giddy. He was ignoring what I'd said about hiding from his friends, but right now, that was fine with me. At least he was willing to have a conversation. "Me, too." I sipped on my pomegranate tea. "I need to tell you about Rupi." I'd tried to bring it up before, but I needed to tell him when we weren't in a crowded hallway or waiting for English class to begin. Now he might actually listen.

"Yeah, what about her?" He downed some coffee.

"You know Esteban, right? Navarro?" I asked.

He nodded.

"Well, I talked to Esteban on Thursday, and he showed me footage that he hacked from the school of Camilla talking to Rupi. Rupi got all mad and stormed off, leaving Camilla alone, crying."

"Camilla was rather private about her love life." Asher munched on a piece of banana bread. "What I knew about their relationship was more from Rupi than Camilla. She's my lab partner in chemistry. I know they were together for a while, though."

"Really? What has she told you?" I finished my tea.

Asher shrugged. "Not much. Most of our exchanges are lab data and pleasantries. She's just said that she misses Camilla. But who doesn't?"

"Why haven't you said anything?"

Asher chewed on his bite of bread and swallowed before saying, "I didn't think much of it. You miss her, and you hardly knew her."

"We gotta talk to her."

Asher rolled his eyes. "If you insist."

Why is he acting weird?

"What? You don't want to?" I placed down my mug. "She might help us make a break in this investigation."

"That's what you say about everything. We've made no progress, unless you count getting the wrong guy arrested." He said the last part in a soft voice, as if he didn't want me to hear.

"*Seriously?*"

"I know you feel strongly about this, but the more we try to find the killer, the more we dig deeper and deeper into a never-ending hole." He reached out to grab my hand on the table, but I brushed it away. "The cops are on it. Besides, like you said, you're off the hook. Nobody's accusing you anymore."

"That's just it. The cops *aren't* on it. They think Mr. Bates did it." I crossed my arms. He'd been encouraging me to show the police the truth about Mr. Bates's innocence, and now he wanted the opposite? "Are you backing out now, Asher?"

"No, no." He shook his head. "Just . . . Forget what I said."

"Well, you said it, so obviously you meant it."

"I didn't know how you would react. I care about you more than I care about halting the investigation."

A smile forced its way onto my lips.

Asher cares about me.

"Fine. Do you have Rupi's contact information?"

"I've had her number since freshman year." Asher took out his phone and dialed. Within a moment or two, a voice sounded on the other side.

Attempting to listen in, I leaned my head toward the phone but only heard Asher.

After he hung up, he cupped my chin in his hands. "She'll be here in five minutes."

"Five minutes? Here?" I'd been trying to get ahold of this elusive girl for two days.

"Yup."

Rupi held a plate with stacked blueberry waffles when she arrived. She was medium-tall and of a muscular stature, and she sat on the opposite side of the booth with a dreary look in her eyes. Her raven hair was tied in a high messy bun, one strand dyed purple. She had a chiseled face with high cheekbones, and maroon pigment painted her lips.

"Hey, Asher. Bexley."

"Thanks for coming." I smiled.

She maintained a straight face, morose. A tight white long-sleeved shirt clung to her upper body, a black crystal necklace hanging over it. I'd promised Esteban that I wouldn't reveal him as the hacker of the school cameras. I knew Asher and Venus would keep the secret, but I didn't know this Rupi girl. How could I bring them up to her without giving Esteban away?

"So, you and Camilla were close?" I continued, hopeful that Rupi would shed some light on what had happened to Camilla.

"I thought so." She hesitated. "Until she cheated on me." Rupi's tone was blatant; the girl didn't seem to hold back the truth. "I can't be mad at her now, can I?" Her sad eyes lingered off in the distance for a few moments.

Wow. "How did you find out? That she cheated, I mean."

The conversation was between Rupi and me; it seemed Asher was more focused on his banana bread than the case.

"She told me."

"I'm sorry." I thought back to the tape; was that what Camilla had been confessing in the footage? "When did she tell you? And how did you react?"

"Whoa, slow down with the questions." Rupi took a deep breath, seemingly thinking about my inquiries. "I was fucking pissed, as any sane human would be. Camilla told me the day of the party. She texted me before, asking to meet at the dining hall. Little did I know, she was preparing to tell me that she was cheating on me." Rupi's eyes became watery as she stared at her untouched waffles. "That was the last time I saw her. I went to the party but avoided her the whole time."

I gave her time to breathe before asking, "Who was she cheating with?"

"She wouldn't tell me." Rupi stabbed her waffles with

her fork—a bit too violently. "I assume now that she'd been talking about Mr. Bates—that murderous creep," she all but spat.

Asher pushed his plate to the middle of the table. "I'm gonna go use the bathroom real quick." He stepped out of the booth. "I'll be right back."

After he was out of earshot, Rupi asked, "So, you and Asher? You two seem cute."

"Oh, I don't know." My relationship with Asher was irrelevant to the case. "Back to you and Camilla, did you . . . have strong feelings against her?"

"Like I said, I was pissed at the time." Rupi gave an incredulous gasp. "Don't you dare suggest—"

"No, never." I pursed my lips. "This case is just impossible to crack."

"What do you mean? Mr. Bates is already arrested."

Oh, right—people still think that.

Rupi put down her fork. "Though I find the whole thing about Eric Fernsby quite strange. A lot of people do. What's going on with that? Do the police think Mr. Bates killed him, too? And if he did, why?"

"I don't know." Wary of trusting anyone, I decided to conceal what I knew from Rupi; she was a stranger, and I had no idea whether she would keep a secret. "This is all so terrible."

Asher returned to the booth, a spaced-out look on his face.

"That was quick."

"Well, I decided I didn't need to use the bathroom after all." He chuckled, mussing his hair. "I think we're done here, no?" Something about him felt off.

"I guess so." Rupi took her stack of waffles—yet to be

eaten—and made for another booth without a goodbye. She was off before I could offer her to stay. She seemed innocent. Then again, things were seldom as they seemed.

Camilla had been cheating on Rupi Khatri. When Camilla confessed, she'd supposedly been talking about Mr. Bates. "Asher?"

"What's up, Bex?"

"Look at the texts." I pulled up the message exchange between Camilla and Mr. Bates. The final text was sent three days before Camilla's murder.

Camilla

What are you gonna
do to stop it? Huh?

"Yeah, what about them?" Asher asked.

"This was three days before. They were obviously in a fight because Camilla wanted to be an elite and threatened to expose him if he wouldn't promise her the spot."

"Yes." Asher furrowed his brows. "We've been over this."

"So why would Camilla admit her relationship with Mr. Bates to Rupi the day of her death? On August 30, they most likely weren't still engaging in their surreptitious affair."

"We don't know that. We shouldn't jump to any conclusions." Asher bit his top lip. "And even if that's true, people are complicated. Camilla could've felt guilty holding it in and wanted to tell Rupi, even if it was no longer occurring. Or the opposite—it could've been the beginning of Camilla's mission to expose him. Then again, she didn't reveal his name, so I don't know if that's plausible."

Why won't you make eye contact with me?

182

I exhaled, realizing my paranoia. "You're right." We weren't getting anywhere.

Asher changed the subject and his facial expression. "What are you doing today?"

"Nothing, really. What about you?"

"Hanging out with you?" He grinned. "What do you say we clear our minds? Forget about the investigation for a little while?"

"That would be nice." I nodded. "Where should we go?"

"My favorite spot?" he asked. "It's pretty during the day, too."

How many times has he gone there? More importantly, how many girls has he brought there?

I shook away the thoughts. "Perfect."

We mirrored each other's positions, leaning over the uneven ledge, watching the day occur beneath us. We had a bird's-eye view of the campus greenery, able to observe students and faculty wandering about Grant Academy's outdoors. We were taller than the trees. Asher kept his lips pursed, his fingers interlocked and resting on the stone. Soft clouds aligned in the sky, hugging one another.

"It's so nice out." I stared up at the blinding sun, squinting at the brightness.

"Yeah." He snickered. His gaze said he had another topic in mind. "Bexley." My name rolled off his tongue like honey. "There's something I kind of want to say. I want us to be on the same page."

"Yes?" My heart hammered in my chest.

Asher heaved an exaggerated breath. "I don't want our relationship to strictly be about the investigation."

The space between us began to feel as if it didn't belong. "Neither do I." My voice sounded small.

"Do you wish you never came here?" he asked after a few beats.

I thought about how much easier life would be if I'd stayed at Vista High. I wouldn't have to worry about catching murderers, having only two people to trust, and ever-expanding heaps of homework.

Yes.

However, I would have to worry about *Abigail*, live with that regret. I'd have to walk the Vista High halls without her next to me. I thought about Asher. The boy who stood beside me was special, irreplaceable, one of a kind. Not to mention, I was so lucky to have Venus. This school—though it held many secrets—was exquisite. The architecture was reminiscent of medieval castles, the type that I'd always dreamed of living in as a child. Every day at the Academy, I felt my brain expand with new knowledge.

"No," I finally answered.

"I'm certainly glad you came." He walked his hand closer to mine on the ledge. "That's just me being selfish." He smiled.

I melted inside, savoring the moment as if it wouldn't last. Asher shrunk the space between us; I eliminated it altogether. The wind picked up, whipping my hair at his cheeks. He chortled, moving away my hair and spitting it from his mouth.

"Sorry."

"Don't be."

As I put up my hair into a ponytail, Asher cleared his throat as if preparing to reveal a secret. "Bexley?"

"Yes?"

"I've had . . . a stupid crush on you since the party." He looked at his fingernails, avoiding eye contact. I'd never seen him so vulnerable, so diffident.

My heartbeat quickened.

"Of course, I couldn't articulate myself very well that night. I made a terrible first impression. Plus, I was frazzled for . . . other reasons," he continued.

"I kind of blocked it from my memory. You don't have to worry there." I touched my lips, wanting his. Feeling my cheeks heat up, I clasped my hands around his nape. Finally, he took his eyes off the floor and lifted them to meet mine.

Millions of contrasting emotions hit me at once. Both of us sat silently, at a loss for words. Nervous heat grew between us.

I blinked, waiting to wake up from this dream, but when I opened my eyes, Asher was still here, dressed in his dumb sweatshirt and silly joggers. Though it wasn't words that floated between Asher and me, a mutual desire overtook us.

With eyelids softly shut, Asher leaned in. He planted a tender kiss on my lips, his hands in my hair.

Sparks flew. Thunder clapped. Lightning surged.

He pulled away after a moment, his eyes full of wonder. Asher licked his lips and took the scrunchy out of my hair, letting my light tresses run loose down his arms.

Yearning for more, I met his lips again. He tasted like rain, like flowers, like everything good in this world. My hands crawled up his back and went under his hoodie, exploring his muscles. Asher pressed his body close to mine. Friction built between us, his heart's pulse echoing on my chest.

He moved his mouth from my lips to my ear and whispered, "I never want to leave." His words clouded dampness on my ear; he was so close to me. My pulse became rapid.

Nothing could ruin this moment.

XIV

*Our doubts are traitors and make us lose the
good we oft might win by fearing to attempt.*
—Shakespeare, *Measure for Measure*

"ONLY THE LIBRARY, I promise."

"Mm-hmm." Venus crossed her arms, eyeing the drawstring that circled around my shoulder. "Why don't you just bring your schoolbag, then?"

"Because . . . Because this one is lighter, and I only need some of my books," I stammered.

Venus lay on her bed, a white faux fur blanket wrapped around her body. "Whatever." She picked up a poetry book—my poetry book—in one hand and her phone in the other: a relaxing way to spend leisure time. "This book is great, by the way, thanks." She waved the book in the air.

"Any time." I'd been around halfway through when she'd taken it from my nightstand and removed the bookmark that held my spot. I wasn't sure if she'd been aware of the fact or cared; sometimes Venus was oblivious in that way, particularly with small-scale happenings that bore little true importance. That trait of hers strangely contrasted with her intent concern for more major matters.

I shuffled out the door of our room, guilt bubbling within me for lying to Venus, my green-and-white plaid dress flowing around me.

It's for the good of the investigation.

I wanted to trust Venus, but I couldn't help considering what Asher had said a little while ago. After all, Venus *had* been the only other person to know about the fire drill. Still, I trusted her alibi.

One foot in front of the other, I started in the direction of Copley House, running my hands along the stucco walls of the hallways. The two other times I'd been there hadn't ended well. I wondered how today would compare.

"The library's in the other direction."

I flinched, turning around to find Venus behind me, her eyes brewing with the sting of betrayal.

"Where are you really off to, Bex?"

Don't tell her. Don't tell her.

But as I looked at Venus, I could sense the innocence that radiated from her. There was no way she could've killed anyone, let alone her friends. "Copley House. I want to prowl around Eric's room, see what I can find."

"Okay." She jogged to my side to catch up.

"You don't have any . . . opinions?"

"Nah." Venus wore black jeans and a yellow tank. "I clearly wasn't invited, so you probably don't want my input."

"I'm sorry. I just—" I started.

"Lied to your best friend?"

What's a good excuse?

"I thought you'd want to stay in and read. Remember? You were really into that book."

"You didn't trust me, did you?"

She was good at reading me. Or I was a bad liar. Or both.

"I think we could find some helpful stuff in Eric's room," I said, dodging the question.

There was a brief pause. "Just one question."

"Yeah?"

"How are we planning on one, not getting in trouble by the school, and two, getting the guys to allow us to surf Eric's bedroom?"

"Good questions." Before the fateful party where Camilla got killed, Venus had been the one urging me to break the rules. That day felt like yesterday yet ages ago all at once. Now the roles had reversed, and I was the one encouraging the mischievous behavior. I was going rogue. "Asher said he'd get his friends out of there. He said they'd never refuse food, so he told them there was some special cookie cake in the dining hall."

"There's cookie cake in the dining hall?" Venus's face lit up.

"Unfortunately, there's not. He said his friends would be livid with him for a few hours after realizing the whole cookie cake thing was a hoax."

"Aw, I love cookie cake," Venus said. "That's so cute. He's willing to make sacrifices for you." She pouted. "Goals."

I could never quite tell if Venus was serious, mocking, or somewhere in between.

It was around half past six when we arrived at the white door of the boys' house. I looked around, making sure no faculty were watching. Hopefully Asher's and my timing aligned, and he and his friends were out of here.

I took Asher's key into Copley from my chain and glided it shakily into the hole. A sigh of relief escaped me as the door seamlessly opened. Unlike the English office incident, I'd come prepared. In the past few days, I'd tried to return to the English office, but there were staff members there during nearly all times of day.

Swinging open the rickety wooden door, I lifted my shoe to find a piece of gum stuck to the bottom. Fabulous.

"Damn, these boys are nasty," Venus said, surveying the room's plastic wrappers and who-knows-what scattered about the syrup-coated floor. "Let's get this over with quickly."

We ascended the stairs and scurried into Eric's room, the location of which I remembered from when I'd been here last: down the hall from the top of the stairs. It seemed untouched, unchanged. The boys must not have known what to do with it since Eric's death. Caution tape blocked the doorway to his room, presumably placed there by the police. His room hadn't been the scene of the crime, but it could conceal potential clues.

Venus and I stepped over the yellow tape, careful not to tear it from the doorway. Eric's plush green velvet comforter covered half of the unmade bed. Above his bed was a bookshelf piled with some classics, breaking at the spines. The room seemed as if he'd left in a hurry just this morning, waking up only a few minutes before the bell for his first class.

He didn't deserve this.

Fishing through my drawstring bag, I found my yellow

gloves. I'd brought a backup in case my first tore or something. I handed the extra pair to Venus.

"Wow, you've come prepared."

"Just in case." I flicked on the light, yet still a sense of darkness and gloom lingered. "Where should we start?"

"I'll check out his closet, you start at the nightstand?" Venus proposed.

"Sounds good."

We tiptoed as if we were top secret spies. Atop his nightstand stood a lamp, some lip balm, and a bottle of lotion—nothing helpful. Each was enclosed in a plastic bag.

Three wooden drawers with iridescent handles were underneath. My hands sweaty beneath my yellow gloves, I pulled open the top one. Inside was a shattered glass frame holding a photograph of Eric with a man and a woman with whom he shared a resemblance. They were probably his parents—the famous ones, though I'd never heard of them. Neither my family nor I had ever been super into comedy shows, so their unfamiliarity made sense.

Why is the frame cracked?

Had he done it, or had it inadvertently fallen? What had his relationship with his parents been like?

Forcing myself back on track, I opened the drawer below. Inside were lone socks. The few that were folded into pairs were mismatched, some pairs of boxers also mixed in. Nothing there.

The last drawer squeaked as it opened. A coarse evergreen blanket that matched the style of Eric's comforter lay folded, though there was a bump at the top.

Is something hidden under here?

I took out the blanket, its neat folds out of place in the otherwise disorganized nature of his room. Nothing. He must've just folded the blanket oddly.

"Find anything?" I asked.

"Nope." Venus cleared her throat. "Maybe we should get out of here before we get caught."

"We can't give up yet." I pushed in the bottom drawer and made for his closet on the other side of the room. As I walked, the floor squeaked beneath me. "Did you hear that?" I said, turning in Venus's direction.

Venus quirked a brow. I took a few steps back and again went over the spot. That certain piece of the wooden floorboard made an eerie noise. It was a stretch, but I kneeled and felt around. The wood blended in so well, it was almost impossible to tell that it wasn't attached to the rest of the floor. Almost.

Slipping my hand into the narrow crevice, I felt the loose piece easily move to the left. Venus moved to my side and helped to lift the piece of wood.

Venus gasped. "No way."

Beneath was a small journal, its exterior a green hardcover. Gold swirls decorated the cover—the two colors of Grant Academy. School spirit.

I tried flipping the front cover open, then realized the lock that circled around it. Chain clinking, I ran my fingers over the parts of the lock. "This is straight out of a movie. It needs some five-letter password."

Venus opened her mouth to speak. Before she could get any words out, the door on the ground floor squeaked open. "Asher, I'mma kill you, bro. You know how much I like cookie cake," Chase's familiar voice blustered, echoing even up here. *Shit.*

"Venus, we gotta get out of here," I whispered, sliding off my gloves as she did the same.

"No kidding." She started toward the door. "There's a back exit in all the group residences. Follow me."

My mindset shifted from wanting to find out about Eric to wanting to avoid getting caught; Asher's friends already weren't fond of me because of last Saturday. As I stood on the threshold after climbing over the caution tape, I looked back and noticed we'd left the wooden piece of the floorboard beside the hole instead of covering it.

There was no time to fix our mistake.

My heart raced as I followed Venus downstairs.

"Venus? Bexley? What are you two doing here?" Chase asked, dressed in an all-black sweatsuit and bouncing a basketball with his un-slinged hand just at the bottom of the stairwell.

"We just . . . Um . . . Venus? Want to tell him why we're here?" I choked out.

"Chill, Suzuki. We're not threatening you or anything." Venus somehow kept her voice from quavering. "I was helping Bexley put a gift in Asher's room. It was supposed to be a surprise, but—"

"Oh, hey guys." Asher stepped toward us. Venus placed a finger over her lips, directed at Chase. "I didn't know you guys were coming." He was a terrible actor. Chase must have been extremely gullible because he snickered and walked away to pass the ball with a friend.

"Well, we're just gonna . . . go now," I said, jogging be-hind Venus toward the exit. The sun was dipping toward the top of a building when we got outside.

"Shoot." I kicked a patch of grass fiercely.

"What?" Venus asked.

"I forgot the journal." My hands clenched into fists by my sides. The whole purpose of the visit was lost; the one thing that could be helpful was gone.

"Turn around."

"Huh?"

"Turn around."

I complied, and she pulled something out from my drawstring: the diary.

"But, how—"

"I stuffed it in your bag before we left."

I exhaled a sigh of relief. "You're the best."

"Tell me something I don't know."

We headed back to the girls' dormitories, eager to examine the journal, or at least try; what could Eric's password possibly be? Venus and I were both at a loss. Perhaps Asher would know.

I texted Asher to come over as I lay with my knit throw blanket.

In a few moments, he responded, saying he'd be over in a few.

He might have thought I was requesting his presence for different reasons, but that hardly mattered. A few minutes passed, filled with Venus and my futile attempts to crack the code of Eric's diary. My phone buzzed.

Asher

Look behind you 😄

I turned around to face my window and found Asher's adorable face peeking through. He wore khaki trousers and a collared white shirt, still in dress code. He probably hadn't had time after class to change.

Venus snickered as I stood on my bed and removed the screening from the window. Asher clambered in, his eyes glowing.

"Bex." After closing the window behind him, Asher pulled me into a tight embrace, joining me on my bed. "I've never seen your room. It's so pretty. Those posters are super cool." He glanced at the woman in front of the Eiffel Tower.

"Yeah. Venus brought them."

"Nice." His gaze shifted to my sketchbook. "This is neat. Can I see it?"

"Um . . ."

Before I could refuse, he began to thumb through the pages, his jaw agape. "Wow, Bex, I didn't know how talented you are."

"Oh, thanks, I guess." I wasn't great at accepting compliments, especially for my art.

He flipped to an old sketch from last November, not far after the night at the lake house. It was a drawing of a girl's body, floating on her stomach atop the water. He couldn't see that. I slammed the cover down, unintentionally smacking his hand with it.

"Ouch."

"We have more important things to worry about than her doodles." Venus sat on her bed with crossed arms, glaring at Asher.

Asher's gaze flicked to Venus. "Oh, Venus, I didn't know you'd be here."

"What? You were expecting alone time?" She laughed. "Sorry about that."

Asher maintained a calm facade, clearly sulking beneath it. "No, I didn't mean it like that."

"Good." She tossed the green-and-gold journal his way, and Asher caught it in midair. "Eric's. Five-letter password. What would it be?" Her words were clipped, direct.

Asher furrowed his brows. "I've never seen this before. You said it belonged to Eric?"

Venus nodded. "We found it—well, Bexley did—hidden under a floorboard."

"Huh."

"Can't you pick the lock or something?" I asked, unsure that we'd be able to come up with Eric's password. After all, there were so many possible combinations.

"Nah. Not this type." He fumbled with the metal loop. "We need a password."

I grumbled. It could be anything.

"Any ideas?" Asher asked.

"Why do you think Bexley texted *you* to come over?" Venus rolled her eyes. "Neither of us has any clue. You were his friend."

Asher ruffled his hair. "I don't know. I guess I'll try some combinations." I looked over his shoulder, watching him arrange the letters.

EricF.

Nothing.

Ferns.

Fail.

Asher.

Nope.

Chase.

Still locked.

Fluff. "His dog," he said.

Again, nothing.

ABCDE.

The lock didn't budge.

Laugh. "His parents' comedy show."

The chain rattled, still locked.

Girls.

Nothing.

Boobs.

"Asher!" I said reprovingly.

"Okay, okay." He groaned. "I'm trying to get creative." He pulled on the lock, but it wouldn't open. "I officially have no idea." Asher flopped back onto my pillow, journal still in hand.

"Try 'Venus.'" She lay on her stomach, holding my poetry book. "You never know."

"Okay."

Venus.

I expected the same outcome as Asher pulled on the lock, but the metal glided open. "Holy shit."

Venus gasped. "I knew he had a crush on me. This better be juicy."

The bell rang.

"Leisure time is over. We have that guest speaker thing, remember? We should come back to this after."

Venus shook her head. "This is much more important. Come on, we can be fashionably late."

I nodded, flipping open to the first page.

THAT ~~GIRL~~ BITCH AT THE TOP OF OUR CLASS ACES
EVERY COURSE.
IN HER, PEERS SEE AN ANGEL; I SEE A WILD HORSE.
IF MERIT DOES NOT DO THE JOB, I'LL REACH THE TOP
WITH FORCE.

TEACHERS FUCKING LOVE HER; GIRLS WANT TO BE HER FRIEND.
THE ONLY THING I DESIRE IS ~~FOR HER LIFE~~ TO FATAL END.
I WILL NOT MAKE A SPECTACLE; LET'S PLAY SOME PRETEND.

DISOWNED BY MY PARENTS, THAT CANNOT BE THE CASE.
ONE CANNOT BLAME ME; THIS SYSTEM IS A RACE.
THERE IS ONE GIRL ON TOP, THAT SHALL BE REPLACED.

I blinked rapidly, in disbelief of the words before my
eyes. My heart thumped wildly.

I NEED THIS HONOR, AS A HUMAN NEEDS FOOD.
IF I DON'T LIVE UP TO MY LEGACY, I'LL BE SCREWED.
CAMILLA HAS SOME SECRETS; I KNOW THAT GIRL'S NO PRUDE.

MY PARENTS' EXPECTATIONS ARE IMPOSSIBLE TO MEET.

DO THEY LOVE ERIC, OR WOULD THEY PREFER A CHEAT?

CAN SHE REALLY BE A GENIUS, POPULAR, AND AN ATHLETE?

His next entry started on the following page.

YOU HIDE ALL YOUR FLAWS, IN AND OUT OF THE CLASSROOM.

NOW FATE WILL SETTLE OVER YOU LIKE A DARK CLOUD

OF DOOM GLOOM.

CAMILLA HARDING, FOR YOU I PREPARE A SPECIAL TOMB.

SHE WEARS TWO FACES; NEITHER SHALL BE AN ELITE.

STEP ASIDE, HARDING. ERIC WILL TAKE YOUR SEAT.

JUST BEFORE ON THE EVE OF THE SCHOOL YEAR, US TWO

WILL MEET.

The last line froze me. The party at which Camilla had been killed was technically on the eve of the school year. I had so many questions. Was *meet* synonymous with . . . *no*. And what were the secrets he mentioned? Did Eric have mere suspicion . . . or more? And if Camilla was so surely going to be an elite, why did she have to beg Mr. Bates for the spot that was already hers? I continued reading, though I wasn't sure I needed to.

YESTERDAY I ~~SAW~~ CAUGHT A GLIMPSE OF CHASE'S SCREEN

AS HE HELPED HIMSELF TO SECONDS OF THE NIGHT'S

FRENCH CUISINE.

THEY HAVE A GROUP CHAT WITH ALL BUT ME. SO MEAN.

RAGE IS BUILDING WITHIN ME LIKE BUBBLES IN A POT.

HEY, MOM AND DAD, I'M A KID . . . NOT A ROBOT.

MY ONLY CHANNEL IS THESE WORDS THAT I JOT.

CAMILLA HIDES EVERYTHING BENEATH A SHEER BAND-AID.

WHAT CLUELESS MORONS MUST POPULATE OUR GRADE.

BY HER ~~NICE GIRL~~ CHARMING FACADE, ONE CAN BE SO

FUCKING SWAYED.

I KNOW I WAS, WHEN IN GOLF PRACTICE WE GREW CLOSE.

THEN SUDDENLY SHE BECAME DISTANT AND MOROSE.

SHE PLAYED ME. I'M PRICKING THE THORNS OF HER ROSE.

GROWING APART IS ONE THING, BACKSTABBING'S ANOTHER.

SHE ALWAYS TOLD ME SHE LOVED ME LIKE A BROTHER.
I SHOWED HER MY HAND, AND SHE PUSHED ME IN THE GUTTER.

Breath heavy, Asher frantically turned to the next page.

WHEN MOM AND DAD SAID, "MAKE A DIFFERENCE," THIS ISN'T
WHAT THEY MEANT.
I STAND AS A DECEIVER, WATCHING MY FRIENDS LAMENT.
HOW, OH HOW, CAN I POSSIBLY REPENT?

That page was stiff with dried tears.

AM I A PSYCHOPATH OR DID I MAKE A MISTAKE?
ALL HUMANS DO, RIGHT? FUCK I'M MY HEART'S GONNA BREAK.
I'M WORSE THAN THEM, WORSE THAN EVERY GAFTG SNAKE.

PLEASE DON'T CRY IN FRONT OF ME AS I TRAIPSE
THROUGH THE HALL.
I'M CRYING BECAUSE FROM MY EYES CURRENTLY POURS A
MASSIVE RAINFALL.
PLEASE SOMEBODY TELL ME THAT SHE DESERVED IT ALL.

"No way." Fear infiltrated my voice. Sweat moistened my cheeks. I thought of the knife that had poked out of his bag during the interview, for "ceramics class."

Asher's lips quivered. "I'm . . . I'm speechless right now. His handwriting, it's real."

"You're sure?"

"Got all his history notes last year. I'm sure. I'll try to find a picture." Sweating, he scrolled through his photos. "I can't find any right now, but you gotta just trust me."

Eric Fernsby killed Camilla Harding.

"I don't want to believe this." Asher wiped away the wetness welling in his eyes. "He was mad at the world. It's my fault, all my friends . . . We were dicks to him." His head dropped.

"What does he mean, he 'showed her his hand?'" I asked.

"I don't know. I . . ." Venus took a deep breath. "Camilla had a way of making people feel close to her, feel comfortable telling her anything and everything. I don't know exactly what he's talking about, but it's probably something about him being vulnerable with her, and her taking advantage of that. I—I don't know." That meant that Eric had been lying when he'd said he and Camilla weren't close.

I remembered the night she rescued me from the closet. In the few minutes I spent with her, I'd already felt her becoming a friend.

"Asher, did you know anything about this?" I turned to him.

He shook his head. "No clue. I just knew they were on the golf team together. I guess they kept their friendship mostly on the course. Even in group settings, I never noticed the two of them seeming super close."

"This is insane. What about Bates? And what in the world are we supposed to do about this?" Venus asked.

I wished I had an answer. "I guess Eric already got his punishment."

Asher shut the diary and threw it across the room, as if touching it burned his hands. His lips—slightly chapped—quivered as he bit back tears. "But who gave it to him?"

XV

Hell is empty and all the devils are here.
—Shakespeare, *The Tempest*

MORALES GLARED FIERCELY at me. "Miss Windsor, hello. You got something for us?"

"Yeah, actually, I do." The little green diary still felt foreign in my hands the day after it'd been found. I pulled it from the pocket of my bomber and placed it gently on the table. We were in the same classroom in which I'd last been questioned. "I've got something of Eric Fernsby's."

Morales reached out hesitantly, flipping open the front cover. She paged through the diary and sat it on her lap. I tapped my foot in anticipation, awaiting a reaction—*Wow, you're amazing!* or *Can we hire you to work for us?*

Instead, Morales arched a brow and said, "You're not a bad poet, dear."

"What do you mean?"

"I mean, the syllables don't match, but the rhymes are impressive."

"You mean *Eric's* rhymes are," I corrected her, trying to hide my unease.

"Where did you even find this?" Morales exhaled and added, "Supposedly."

"It was in his room. Beneath the floorboard. This was Eric's, I swear it."

"Mm-hmm. Floorboard. Classic." Morales crossed her arms, looking amused. "So you broke into Eric's room, which was guarded off with caution tape?"

"I . . . Does that really matter?" I asked. I should've come up with a story, a way in which the diary miraculously showed up in my hands. Still, how could she refute such perfect evidence? That was just it—because of how perfect it was.

"Yes. Yes, it does. And now that you pulled this, the texts from Mr. Bates's computer don't seem too promising." Morales leaned forward so I could feel her breath. "You do know there are serious consequences for lying to the police and tampering with evidence, right?"

"Of course, but—"

"We did cross-check sources about Camilla and Mr. Bates's affair. Still, I'm gonna keep an extra eye on you." Her burning gaze forced me to look away.

"Here, do you have a sheet of paper? I'll write something right now to show you that isn't what my handwriting looks like," I offered.

Reluctantly, Morales fished through her briefcase and pulled out a crumpled piece of scrap paper. "Copy down the first stanza."

She opened the diary up to the page for me, though the words were already ingrained in my mind. I began to write.

"All right, but it's not hard to disguise your letter—"

"I'm trying to help." Suddenly, the diary seemed less like a weapon and more like a curse. "I guess you guys don't want it." I was done with Morales; nothing I could do would please her. Grumbling, I grabbed the diary, but she tugged it back.

"We'll be keeping this. Mr. Bates may be arrested for sexual activity with a student, but this case isn't closed. And hey, stay out of this trouble. Seriously," she warned.

"Fine." I stomped away and slammed the door behind me.

The next Monday, lying on my stomach on my unmade bed, I aimlessly scrolled through Instagram. The more and more I thought about Eric, other ideas sprang to mind: What if the diary had been planted there? Then again, it had been beneath the floorboard, and Asher had said it matched Eric's handwriting. Classical music played in my ears; the waltz that Asher had shown me brought a grin to my face. It dimmed when the truth dawned on me for what seemed like the fortieth time today: Eric was a cold-blooded murderer, and now he was dead.

I searched "Eric" in Venus's following. Two accounts came up: @ur.hyst_eric_al and @ericfernsby. I pressed the first one—thirty-four followers and no profile photo. The bio said "finstagram." The other account had 928 followers and was public. His profile picture showed him in a hoodie in front of a sunset, his hands in his pockets, his gaze to the side. The picture was on Grant's campus; I recognized the cedar trees in the background. All his bio said was "GAFTG."

His most recent post was a group picture from June last year. Chase, Camilla, and he sat on a couch, the lighting dim. Emojis covered what I assumed to be a vape in Chase's hand. Eric looked happy.

I clicked on the comments. Most were from June, but a bunch were recent. "RIP bro." "Rest easy my boy." "We love you."

A lump formed in my throat. He was dead, but he was a murderer. I didn't know whether to despise him or pity him. Both, perhaps.

Eric's mom and dad sandwiched him in the next post. They sat on a gray couch with a green screen behind them, probably on set for their show, their stiff and waxy smiles looking fake. As I lay wondering what Eric's parents thought now, an alarming email popped up on my phone.

Dear Miss Bexley Windsor,

Attached below are your month one grades.

Sincerely,
The Academy Staff

Esteban's words came to mind: *The staff switched the system to showing us our grades month by month.* I wasn't sure whether to thank him or hate him for it; I'd been frequently skipping classes, looking for answers in the investigation where they didn't exist.

Why did I care about the case so much? For my own peace of mind? For Abigail? Mr. Bates was imprisoned for a crime he hadn't committed. My opinions on Eric were conflicting; he was a murderer, yet he'd gotten punishment for his wrongdoing. The biggest question still remained: Who was the one to punish him?

I was too deep into the case to surrender now. Neither Asher nor Venus cared as much as I did; each day they seemed to drift away more and more from the investigation. Asher always subtly changed the subject when I brought it up, and Venus would put in her headphones and start listening to a podcast, blatantly ignoring me.

Education wasn't going anywhere. Solving this investigation was imminent to my sanity. Even if people no longer thought it was me, I wasn't one to let things like this go so easily—*not after Abigail.*

Bracing myself, I scrolled down to the file attachment on the email labeled *Month One Report, Bexley Windsor.*

> European History: B–
> Calculus: B
> Latin 12: B+
> Physics: B–
> Shakespearean Literature: C+
> Physical Education: A

My lips began to quiver.

How had I done so poorly? A C-plus in English? I'd thought Mr. Trist liked me or at least was willing to go easy on me as I was a new student. In the first two weeks of school, I'd worked tremendously hard to keep up with each class. It seemed everything had fallen apart since then.

Ditching classes will do that.

All those skips hadn't even been worth it; since the discovery of the diary with Asher and Venus, no more breakthroughs had been made in the case—probably because I'd been trying to work alone. All the best advances we'd made happened when we worked as a team. It was clear both of them were no longer as into the case as I was. Besides, my paranoia whispered slightly, *What if I can't trust them?*

These grades were so unlike me. Back at Vista, school had been a breeze. I'd received consistent A's and A-pluses. Now physical education was my best class, and *everyone* got an A in gym; the coaches were lazy with grading.

Just then, a second notification appeared on my phone: an email from Mr. Trist.

Hello Bexley,

As I'm sure you've noticed with the posting of September grades, it appears you've begun to fall behind in my Shakespearean Literature class. You've been marked absent for the last three classes, and your Shakespeare analysis paper was due last Wednesday.

Are you all right? I'm quite concerned.

All the best,
Mr. Trist

My hands clenched into fists. Naturally, I wondered what grades other people had gotten. Had Jessie succeeded in English? What about Asher?

I shook away the thoughts. This wasn't a competition. Except that it was.

The whole concept of the elite system was inherently competitive, just as Eric had mentioned in his diary. Compared to all the other students in my grade, I was hardly in the running to become an elite. Still, I wanted to at least do well—my best, if not for the school's best. For Mom and Dad. I'd never show them these grades. They'd be so disappointed.

I began typing an email back to Mr. Trist.

Mr. Trist—

> This past week has been very hectic for me. I understand that my priorities have been distorted. I'm so sorry for my negligence. If you'd be available to meet with me sometime soon, that would be extremely helpful.
>
> Kind Regards,
> Bexley

Knock, knock, knock.

His door was open. Still, common courtesy told me to knock.

Mr. Trist gestured me in with an inquisitive gaze. "Bexley, thanks for coming in."

"Thank you for letting me."

Mr. Trist cleared his throat and gestured for me to take a seat beside him. "Let's cut to the chase, Miss Windsor."

"Of course." I stepped over the threshold, gazing out the window and watching the sun hide behind the fluffy white clouds. "I'm really sorry."

"Don't be sorry. Do tell me what's going on with you." Mr. Trist put on glasses, as if doing so would allow him to see through me.

"I've just been . . . distracted."

"Is it about the murders?" he asked, as if he already knew the answer.

I nodded, picking at the side of the wooden table. "The investigation has been keeping me up at night. It's so hard to get anything else done." It felt good to tell the truth, even if only a small part of it.

"Don't worry, Bexley. David Bates is locked up for what he did. The Academy is safe from him now," Mr. Trist said. "It's a real shame, though. I liked the man a lot—before I knew what he did, of course. Though I do wonder what will happen with his trial. I heard he's hired a fine lawyer."

"I guess."

"You guess what?"

"That . . . everything's fine."

"Is there something you're not telling me?" Again, his rhetorical tone made it seem as if he already knew there was.

"No, no. Nothing like that."

"You don't think Bates did it, do you?" Mr. Trist tapped the eraser cap of his pencil on the mahogany table. "Why is that?"

My stomach lurched. Why would he ask me this? "What? I—Yeah, he did, right?" I said, nonplussed. Heat rushed to my cheeks.

"Bexley, I'm a teacher. You can and should trust me. If you know something, you've got to tell me." Mr. Trist tilted his chin downward, revealing his eyes above his glasses.

"About the essay, should—"

"Tell me, Miss Windsor. Do you know something about the murder of Camilla and Eric?" he persisted.

"No." In fact, I really didn't know—about *Eric's* murder, anyway. "I also don't know what this essay is supposed to be ab—"

"What have you been doing instead of attending English class?" Mr. Trist's tone turned from friendly to reproachful.

"Really, I've been distracted. I get lost sometimes within this huge campus, and the schedule confuses me."

He scratched his bald head. "Is that right, Miss Windsor?"

"Please, I came here to get help on this essay."

Mr. Trist smirked, scratching the scruff on his chin. "Right, right. Apologies. You can pick any of Shakespeare's sonnets to analyze in a well-written essay. Anywhere between one thousand to fifteen hundred words is fine. I'll expect it double-spaced and printed on my desk tomorrow."

"Tomorrow?"

"By noon." He cleared his throat for what felt like the tenth time. "Unless, of course, you have something to tell me."

"I'll see you tomorrow, Mr. Trist, with the essay. Thanks again for letting me come in."

It seemed people were seldom honest and genuine at the Academy—finally, I found one way I fit in. I managed a stilted smile before gathering my belongings and escaping the classroom. Studying the paintings on the hallway walls, I thought about my conversation with Mr. Trist. His words seemed so unlike him.

"Yo, Bexley." It was Chase, leaning against the wall with arms crossed.

I flinched as he approached me. "What's up?"

His usual calm demeanor was absent, replaced with a scowl. "Planting a gift in Asher's room, were you?"

"What are you talking ab—"

"You and Venus mysteriously poking around our house? There was no gift. Only a piece of Eric's floorboard out of place." His hands clenched into fists. "And your little boyfriend won't tell me shit," he spat, a scowl across his face.

"What's it to you?"

He laughed mockingly. "What's it to me? *What's it to me?*" There was an edge to his voice, and it seemed as if he was resisting the urge to punch me in the face. "Eric was my close friend, and you keep prowling around where you aren't wanted. What's your problem, anyway?"

"*My* problem? You're the one who came here to scold me when I did nothing wrong. Why don't you take it up with Venus? She was there, too." I tried to keep my composure.

"I've known Venus for years. I trust her. You, on the other hand . . . Things at Grant have been perfect for all my years here. You show up as a senior, and suddenly two of my best friends are gone?" He shook his head. "I haven't figured you out yet, but when I do—"

"I get it. I really do. Losing a best friend hurts. And I'm so sorry that you had to go through it twice. If I could bring them back, I would."

"I don't believe you." The anger in his voice faded to only gray hopelessness. It was infectious.

"You don't have to. I just hope you know that I'd never do anything to harm someone." *Not on purpose.* "You don't need to like me, but please believe that my concern to solve this case is fueled by nothing other than genuine concern and empathy."

"Then why the fuck do you care so much? Why did you break into Eric's taped off room?"

"I'm sorry, Chase. I've got to go." It was time for calculus.

As I sauntered off, I wondered. Chase had said his broken arm was from an arm wrestle. Eric had died in a fistfight. When I thought about it more, I remembered how Jessie had thrown the drink in his face. He'd gotten up after that, and that was the last I saw him that night. Did Chase simply care dearly about his friend, or did he have something to hide?

For days, I threw myself into school, the case a mere afterthought. When the one-year anniversary of Abigail's death approached, I pushed away the memories. I scrambled to write a twelve-hundred-word essay, practiced math problems from the textbook, and watched a history documentary that'd been assigned a week prior.

I couldn't do this without Asher and Venus passionately on the same page, and right now, they weren't. So many questions remained up in the air, the answers seeming galaxies away, if they even existed. In calculus and physics, there was always one right answer. I followed a formula that led me to a definitive solution. That was my favorite part of school. I could rely on something. So I did. For days. I wasn't late to a single class, and my test scores soared into the high nineties. *Academics* was practically in the title of Grant Academy—the reason I'd come, and I couldn't forget that.

Well, one of the reasons.

October 17, 12:58 a.m.

Last Year

ABIGAIL RAN HER fingers along the rim of her glass—her fourth one of the night. She loved the way the vodka burned her throat and turned her mind all fuzzy.

Bexley's lake house overlooked the waves, navy blue and violent tonight. The Windsors shared the house with their cousins. Her parents had finally agreed to let her and Abigail have the house to themselves while they visited Cape Cod for a college friend's wedding.

Bexley took one last sip and slammed the empty glass onto the marble kitchen countertop. "We're so pathetic," she said, words slurred.

Abigail giggled. Her auburn hair hung half up, half down, freckles scattered across her face. She wore a paisley halter top and leather pants for no other reason than to sit beside Bexley and sip on her parents' alcohol. "I want to do something daring tonight." Abigail fingered a piece of Bexley's blond hair, first looping it around, then giving it a single hard tug.

"Me too. We could prank call people."

"Could you be any lamer?" Abigail meant it playfully, but Bexley felt her heart sink a bit. "We should go for a swim."

"It's freezing out." Bexley gazed out the window, eyeing her parents' speedboat. Before speaking the thought, she turned it down; they would kill her.

Abigail gasped. "The boat! Is that what you're looking at?" she asked. "Little Bexley has a good idea for once."

"Nah. It's already dark, and I don't even know how to drive it." Bexley tried not to dwell on Abigail's condescending words.

"I do. I interned at summer camp and drove kids for bumper tubing, remember?" Abigail was already midway up the stairs to Bexley's bedroom. "I'm getting changed, then we'll go?" Though she posed it as a question, Bexley knew better than to think it was optional.

Bexley donned a dark purple bikini with high-waisted bottoms and threw on her Vista High sweatshirt. It was uncomfortable but did its job to keep her warm.

Abigail unlatched the door a little, yet the wind swung it fully open and welcomed air into the lamplit kitchen. A breeze swam its way behind Bexley's ear and down her spine. The water summoned them forth.

The speedboat was white, decorated in green and gray, but tonight it was all just darkness. Bexley trembled behind Abigail on the wooden dock.

"Let's go," Abigail said as she climbed into the boat.

"I don't know where the keys are," she said, climbing in after Abigail. "Probably around here somewhere. I'm not sure where."

"You search the front, I got back."

After five minutes of no keys, Bexley sighed. "Let's just go back."

Abigail shook her head, her silhouette outlined by the glinting moonlight. She was so tall and slender. "I didn't put on this bathing suit for nothing."

"I don't—"

"What if we use that boat instead?" Abigail cocked her head toward the adjacent speedboat, which shared the same shape and characteristics. "It's my birthday in two days. Please?"

"That boat belongs to the Weinsteins," Bexley said, already knowing she wouldn't win.

"It's"—Abigail clicked on her phone—"1:17 in the morning. The Weinsteins are probably asleep. We'll have it back to them before they wake up."

Bexley glanced in the direction of the Weinsteins' house. The lights were all out. "If you can find the key."

Abigail squealed, hopped out of the boat, and ran along the dock to the Weinsteins' boat. Bexley followed, cursing under her breath as she saw the keys, shiny in the blackness of night. They sat unassumingly on the cushion before the wheel.

"Bingo!" Abigail whisper-screamed, lunging for the keys and then jangling them in her hands. "Sit back, relax, and enjoy the ride." She grinned back at Bexley, her phone flashlight on her lap, casting light upward at her face—a vision that would haunt Bexley in the future. "We are so not lame."

Bexley unhooked the boat from the rope at the dock. "Stupid, maybe a little. Lame, definitely not." She was shivering, and it wasn't only from the cold.

Abigail took the wheel in her hands and sped them into the forbidden horizon. Bexley sat beside her friend and let her hair smack her face.

"We just stole a boat. Abigail, how did we just do that?" she shouted over the motor noises, alcohol floating in her system.

"We just stole a fucking boat!" repeated Abigail. "We just stole a . . . What did we do? Bexley, what did we just do? Wait, how do you turn this thing?" Her tone shifted.

"What the hell? Turn it! I thought you knew how to drive a boat." She'd known this was a bad idea. Why would she—

Abigail erupted into an obnoxious guffaw. "That was priceless! Should've seen your face."

"What? Abigail, what the hell?"

"I was *messing* with you. It was a *joke*. Ever heard of that?" Abigail turned to look at Bexley, who was biting her fingernails.

"Okay, fine. Let's just—keep your eyes on the road. I mean, the water. Just go for a few minutes, then we'll turn back." Bexley's teeth began to chatter. It was frigid.

"Are you crazy?" Abigail took one hand off the wheel. "This is euphoria. This is the dream. This is—you know what this is? This is what life is about." Her words were wavy.

Bexley shoved Abigail's hand back on the wheel and muttered profanities.

"Want to try it out?" Abigail offered. Her red hair was flying every which way.

"No, thank you."

Abigail shrugged. "Suit yourself. Woohoo!" she screamed. She was laughing so hard, Bexley couldn't hear herself think. At least one of them was having fun. It continued like that for a few minutes, Abigail having the time of her life.

Bexley put her hands in the air; maybe if she feigned enjoyment, it would come. As the wind picked up, Abigail laughed, veering the boat to the left. Bexley's hand slammed against the hard boat.

"Ow," Bexley moaned. She felt as if her knuckle had cracked in half. That would leave a scar.

"What happened?" Abigail shouted. "You good?"

"Let's go back. Please. I think I just broke something in my hand."

"You'll be fine, drama queen." Abigail quickly resumed her euphoric cheering. Bexley had yet to see the day she would finally stand up to Abigail.

At once, a noise, similar to the boat's motor, seemed to be coming from behind them.

"Abigail, be quiet for just a second," Bexley urged, putting a hand on Abigail's arm.

"Rude." But she did, and they both heard it. There was another boat behind them. They called out on a megaphone. It was the lake security police.

XVI

Doubt thou the stars are fire;
Doubt that the sun doth move;
Doubt truth to be a liar;
But never doubt I love.
—Shakespeare, *Hamlet*

I STARED UP at the ceiling, observing every nuance, every brushstroke of the stucco. Lavender aromatic air emanated from my diffuser. It was supposed to lull me to sleep, yet my body was awake as ever.

"The details of Eric's death are so garbled." I flipped my pillow over, hoping the other side would be crunchy and cold.

I tried to run over the potential suspects in my head, but nothing seemed plausible. It didn't add up that Brandt's note seemed to be from the same person who'd murdered Camilla, yet he'd received it after Eric died.

The hour was way past my usual bedtime, yet sleep eluded me—my mind, that is; fatigue easily overtook my body.

"Why don't we forget about this for a little while?" Venus muttered, half asleep.

"Forget?"

"We're clearly not getting anywhere." She adjusted her sheets. "We've discussed this ad nauseam."

Her words sounded strangely like Asher's. Had they discussed their desires to halt the investigation?

"Are you kidding? We can't give up now."

"Says who, Bex?"

"We're so close. Don't you want to find the murderer once and for all?"

"We already know that it was Eric."

"But what about *his* murderer?"

Her tone turned cold. "His murderer was giving Camilla justice." Venus stifled her yawn. "Count me out of this. I don't want to spend all my time on this case anymore."

"What are you saying?" I squeezed my pillow, taking out my exasperation on it as opposed to letting my feelings show in my voice.

"I just told you. I'm sick of this case. I don't understand why you're so invested. All I ever wanted was to find Camilla's murderer, and we have."

"Why?" The fire drill . . . her recent avoidance of the case . . . and why was her name the password to Eric's journal? What if she'd planted the journal? What if she'd lied about her August 30 alibi, and that was the real reason she didn't want me to tell anyone? "You have something to hide?" The words left me before I could think.

Venus paused. "The fact that you would even say something like that . . ." Her voice was different. Hurt. I'd never heard her speak like that.

"I . . . I didn't mean . . ." But the words were out there,

floating uncomfortably between us, and I couldn't wish them back. "Good night."

She didn't respond.

His fervent touch was a drug, and I was hooked. "It's okay, Bex." Asher's arms circled loosely around my waist. "Shh, it's all gonna be okay."

I lay on my side, facing Asher's blank wall, his arms wrapped around me from behind. We were supposed to be back in our own dorms, but by following that protocol, I'd have to face Venus and the regret that came with that. I'd avoided her all day since the tension last night. Now, it was much past curfew. "I'm sorry."

"Don't be." He ran his fingers through my tangled hair. "Tell me what's wrong."

"No, it's just—I feel like everything is falling apart. Venus is sick of the case. So am I, but I'm not going to give up. Not when we've already come this far."

"What happened?"

I shut my eyes, tuning out the barbaric chatter of his friends, muffled through the doorway. "I kinda . . . almost accused her of hiding something." I winced as the words escaped me.

"You what?"

"Remember what you said about the fire drill? That Venus could've tried to frame me?" I said, turning over to face him.

Asher nodded, placid.

"Well, I was close to confronting her. I think she could tell."

"I'm sure you're overthinking it." Asher tickled my shoulders. "What did she say?"

"Nothing really. A little offended, that's all." I hesitated; the near argument with Venus made me think of Abigail. "I haven't told anyone the reason I came here senior year." It wasn't exactly the answer to his question. Still, it was important for me to get it off my chest. "My best friend, Abigail, passed away in autumn of last year." I remembered finding out. The way the phone had dropped from my hands, the screen shattering. "They never found out what happened to her. But she was missing one night"—I sniffled—"and her body was found under a dock the next morning." Telling myself that story so many times made it seem like the truth. Like I was the good guy.

Asher didn't say anything, but his soft embrace communicated all I needed to know; he was there, understanding.

"I never tried to find out what happened to her because I was scared." I bit my lip, trying to stop the noises of despair that poured from my lips. "I thought that maybe, with Camilla and Eric, I could get them the justice that they deserved—the justice that Abigail deserved but never got."

"Wow, Bex, I'm sorry. I never knew," he said, shaking his head, genuine concern in his eyes.

"You wouldn't have."

"Do you want to talk about it?" he asked, his voice delicate.

I shook my head. "Not really."

He nodded. "We should dress up together."

"That was an abrupt change of subject."

"You shouldn't dwell on what you can't control. You and Venus will reconcile the relationship."

But I wasn't so sure. "Fine. Dress up? What do you mean?"

"For Halloween. We could do, like, a couples' costume."

A couples' costume would imply that we were . . . a couple. "A *what* costume?"

"I mean, *are* we a couple?" Asher's cheeks flushed. "Do—do you want to be?"

My heart twinkled. "I'd love that." I tousled his hair with my hands. "What would the costumes be for, though? You said you didn't want to go to the party."

He shrugged. "For us." Asher's watch read quarter to ten. "The night is young. Do you wanna go somewhere? Take a respite?"

I nodded.

"There's a huge costuming room that they use for all the productions."

"You wanna sneak around?" I asked, quirking a brow.

Asher grinned with a sinister spark in his cavernous eyes. His brown waves lay like a beautiful yet messy nest on his head.

"I'd be okay with that." I wiped away the tears that no longer belonged on my cheeks. "But there's one thing I want to do first."

Our bodies pressed close together, I leaned in to meet his lips. His hands went to the small of my back, my skin tingling beneath his touch. My tongue mingled with his.

Asher pulled back to ask, "Do you want—"

The door flew open, and Chase entered, oblivious, the familiar black sling around his arm. "Yo, Ash, we're having some ice cream downstairs if—" Asher quickly removed his hands from my body and jerked up from his bed. Chase looked at us, and his uncovered hand leapt to cover his mouth. "Shit, sorry guys." He scurried out the door.

"Sorry about that." Asher sat on the edge of his bed. "Shall we resume?"

"Another time," I said, no longer feeling comfortable to go on with him in a house filled with people. "That costuming place you were talking about—should we go now?"

Asher beamed. "Let's go."

Similar to the time when we snuck into Mr. Bates's classroom, our phone flashlights were our main light sources, and Asher's ran out of battery within a few minutes of walking through the silent campus.

We soon arrived at a creaky wooden door. The costuming room was gloomy and unlocked, as Asher said it usually was. Asher flicked on the lights once we arrived, snickering at our devious ways.

Does everyone break the rules?

"This room seems old."

"It is."

There was hardly any room to breathe, dresses and accessories filling every corner of the space. Even with the lights on, the room was dim. Hangers lined the walls in disorganized rows.

"No offense, but why would we come here?" I asked.

"You don't think it's magical?" Asher reached out and grabbed an outfit of metal armor. "I remember seeing this knight piece in one of the plays last year."

"Knight and day?"

"Pardon?"

"For Halloween, we could be night and day, only an actual . . . *knight* costume." I laughed.

"We could do sun and moon, or something with stars, or . . ." His eyes wandered about the hefty closet. "There's Beauty and the Beast . . . Snow White and the Prince."

"And we're allowed to just take costumes at our heart's content?"

"*Allowed* is a strong word." Asher chuckled. "But the costuming people are pretty forgetful. They only come in this room when they're looking for clothing for a play—they most likely won't notice a few missing pieces." He held up a hanger with a beautiful yellow ball gown, designed with pearls and puffy cap sleeves. "Besides, we'll return them after."

"Oh my goodness, that's stunning. Is that for Belle from *Beauty and the Beast*?" The beads sparkled with the yellow fabric. "That duo will be easy—you won't have to dress up," I teased.

"Bexley!"

"I'm kidding, I'm kidding." I stood on my tippy-toes to plant a kiss on Asher's soft lips. "It might be hard to be the beast. How about you dress up as what the beast looked like after the transformation?"

"So, you mean the prince?"

"Exactly." I took the hanger with the yellow dress from his hand and twirled around, holding it to my body.

He grabbed a hanger with a blue embroidered tunic. "We should put them on."

"Okay." I giggled. "Turn around."

Asher whipped his head the other direction respect-fully and observed the other pieces as I undressed and stepped into the beautiful yellow dress.

"Can I look yet?"

"One sec." I pulled up the heavy gown so the sweet-heart neckline began right below my neck. "Okay, you can turn."

Asher gasped as he gazed up and down. "You're gorgeous."

"Will you tie the corset for me?"

He nodded and threaded the ribbon through the cor-set holes. "This dress was made for you, Bex." His fingers brushed against my back, sending shock waves through my entire body.

I grinned. "Your turn. Try on the prince suit."

In a few minutes, we were matching in our Beauty and the Beast costumes. "This is hysterical. Here, Bex, take a picture." He handed me his phone. "The password is five-nine-six-six."

After taking the photo, I said, "We have to wear these for Halloween," as I ran my hands over Asher's prince outfit, admiring the different textures.

"I'm down. It'll be a great night."

I smiled. "Unforgettable."

XVII

Love looks not with the eyes, but with the mind,
And therefore is winged Cupid painted blind.
—Shakespeare, *A Midsummer Night's Dream*

T HE MOMENT MY phone read *October 31,* the air
froze in my lungs.

Brandt's note.

I'd forgotten about it ever since that night with Asher.
All my thoughts had been concerning him and schoolwork, leaving no spare brainpower for the investigation.
Every exchange with Venus these past few weeks had felt
strained, like we both suspected each other. We shared
occasional hellos and goodbyes, but no more meaningful
conversations.

Today was Halloween, the day that had for a while felt
so distant. Shakespearean Literature was first period. The
bell would ring in five minutes.

I hurried out of bed, quickly tied my hair up, and
threw on my pun Halloween costume for the school day:

a yellow dress with a *Life* nametag and a basket of lemons. *When life gives you lemons.* Asher was going to be lemonade.

Venus snored away the morning hours in her bed; she had first period free.

If only things could be normal between us again.

These last few weeks, I'd become better at attending classes, and on time. I hadn't ditched a class since my meeting with Mr. Trist; that appointment had been an excruciating experience that I had no desire to repeat.

I slipped out the door silently—careful not to wake Venus—and headed down the corridor. Outside the girls' dorms, Asher stood, his schoolbag swung over one shoulder. "Good morning, Bex."

"Hey there, lemonade." He wore a yellow striped tee, gray sweatpants, and a sticker that read *Lemonade*. "You couldn't be more creative?"

"Neither I nor any of my friends own yellow pants. What was I supposed to do? Besides, I wanted to take advantage of the one non–dress code day and wear sweats."

"At least you tried. Have you been waiting out here for me?" I pecked his lips, and my insides tingled. "You didn't have to do that."

"I wanted to." Asher grinned. "Besides, I was on the phone with my dad for most of the time."

"Oh, fun." We headed toward Sodmeyer Hall as many students milled about. Through the windows, I could see that trees had lost most of their leaves. "What were you guys talking about? Or, you don't have to say, of course."

"No, no, I will. He was just telling me about some news with his company, mostly about his merch."

"Oh, right, his plumbing company. You told me about that."

"Yeah. He *loves* to send me merch—clothes, pens . . . Sometimes he sends me the strangest things, like a comb or even a vase. One time he sent me fake nails." Asher chuckled.

"Hey, I'd love some fake nails." I nudged his arm. Entering the building, I brushed my fingers across the *Halloween party* flyers, surprised the school allowed them. A jack-o'-lantern sporting a witch hat flashed a spooky grin in the center.

"Okay, but do you want them to say 'McCoy Plumbing' in bright orange? Yeah, that's what I thought," he said.

As we entered Mr. Trist's classroom, Jessie shot me a nasty glare. I'd recently gotten better at not taking it personally. She was just jealous. If she knew everything that went on in my head, would she still be? If she knew about the depression that losing Abigail had driven me into for so long, would she still be?

"So, students," Mr. Trist's voice boomed, "today we'll be reading some *Othello* and then critiquing a mystery student's essay as a class."

The bell sang, officially commencing the class period. The last students trickled in through the doorway.

"Books out, everyone. Who would like to be our Iago?"

My hand shot up, as I was desperate for extra class participation points.

"Yes, Bexley, you can go from where we left off yesterday."

I nodded, tracing the words with my pencil. "Oh, villainous!" I exclaimed, putting my acting skills from last year's school play to use. "I have looked upon the world for four times seven years, and since—"

"I have a question," Jessie interrupted, drumming her lacquered fingernails on the dark wooden tabletop.

Invisible beneath the table, my hands curled into fists. "You could have waited until I was finished with the passage." Finally, I was beginning to find the courage to stand up for myself.

Seeming to ignore me, Jessie said, "Why would he say four times seven? Why couldn't he just say twenty-seven?"

If she was going to interrupt, she should at least know simple math. "You mean twenty-eight?" I corrected.

"No, twenty-sev—oh, yeah, twenty-eight." She rolled her eyes, her cheeks flushing. "Why would he say his age like that, though?"

"It's just the way they spoke back then, Jessie." Mr. Trist's voice was full of pent-up annoyance.

"Okay, then I guess I'm six times three." Jessie's *Othello* book wasn't even open; she leaned her pale elbows on the cover.

"Yeah, and I'm seven times two plus five minus one," another student chimed in. The class exploded into giggles.

"Enough!" Mr. Trist yelled, his change in tone alarming. "You do realize that I recommend students to the elite board, right?" Those simple words halted all the laughter and side chatter. "We'll come back to *Othello* later. Let's transition into the essay critique, since clearly you guys have the giggles."

He walked over to his computer and pulled up "Sonnet 138." "Now, in order to understand the student's essay, we'll first read the sonnet on which it is based. As reading aloud has demonstrated itself to be catastrophic, please read in your heads."

My eyes skimmed over most of it, but something about the ending pulled me in. Most of it was gibberish to me, except for the last few unsettling lines . . .

> O love's best habit is in seeming trust,
> And age in love loves not t' have years told.
> Therefore I lie with her, and she with me,
> And in our faults by lies we flattered be.

Next period, I fidgeted my way through history class, a lesson about mutually assured destruction—how one military power would hold back a nuclear attack lest they were not met with a dangerous counterattack. But for the whole period, my mind was occupied with other matters.

Asher tied up the corset of my new favorite yellow dress. I'd curled my hair for the first half of leisure time and dabbed on some makeup to make myself more fit for the stunning gown.

"You're a true vision," Asher said. "Stunning."

Heat rose to my cheeks. "You're not too bad yourself."

His single dimple made my heart sing. "What do you want to do? The night is ours."

"I don't know. Would you want to go for a walk? Around campus, maybe?" I proposed.

"Eh, I don't know about wandering around campus, especially with that note you told me about."

"Oh, right. I didn't think of that. I guess we could stay here in Copley, then." A pang of guilt hit me; Brandt was probably expecting me to join him at the party.

Asher brushed his fingertips against my cheeks. "I wouldn't complain."

I giggled. "So, before we went into Shakespearean Lit, you were in the middle of telling me something? Your dad's company?"

"Oh, right." Asher gave one last tug on the corset ribbons and let go. "That was pretty much all. The amount of 'McCoy Plumbing' orange things I have is insane. He sends me packages and packages of merch. Still, I always get excited when they arrive. It's not much, but at least I know he's thinking of me."

Orange things?

Asher stood regally beside me before the mirror, interlacing his fingers through mine. I adored our reflection. "Prince and princess," he said, his face dashing.

Oh my goodness. Oh. My. Goodness.

No. No. No, no, no.

"Bex, what's wrong?" He blinked at me in the mirror.

I thought of the note that Brandt had received, written in orange ink.

Anyone could have orange pens.

But nobody regularly used orange pens. Red, blue, black, even green or purple—*not orange.*

The line from class today came to mind.

O love's best habit is in seeming trust.

I recalled my first date with Asher, when he'd shown me his leather-bound journal of suspects. There'd been a quote scrawled on the last page: "When devils will the blackest sins put on / They do suggest at first with heavenly shows / As I do now." Back then, I hadn't thought much of it, but the idea had lingered in the back of my mind.

He's a liar. The one person who's supposed to be here for me.

Asher planted a kiss on my lips. I falsely reciprocated.
"What's wrong? You look . . . unsure of something."

"No, nothing." Our tongues swam together. If he was
actually dangerous, I couldn't confront him; I had to put
on an act. As his hands roamed my body, I fought the
urge to slap them away.

"I'm gonna go use the bathroom real quick, okay,
Bex?" He pulled away and kissed my forehead before escaping through his door. As soon as he left, I wiped the
filthy taste of his lips from my mouth. I'd been deceived
by the only person I had left.

Holding up the skirt of my yellow ball gown, I raced to
his desk drawer. In it lay a pencil case. My hands trembled
as I unzipped it, beads of sweat forming on my forehead.
Lo and behold, orange pens filled the case. Heartbeat fast,
I grabbed his phone from his nightstand.

What else is he hiding?

Panicked and with little time, I remembered his password from the other day.

Five-nine-six-six.

I searched up Brandt Harding in his text messages.
Nothing popped up.

Battling the nervous spasms overtaking my body, I
typed in Eric, and a long chain of messages appeared.
That wasn't surprising; they'd been friends.

Eric

Free next period?

Yup

I scrolled up, nothing too startling appearing.

> Come downstairs for breakfast.

Eric
Coming

Check out this vid.
LMAO.

> hahahhahahha

Eric
This dude never misses.

Their messages didn't seem to hold any red flags. Quickly, I searched Camilla's name in his text messages. Asher's footsteps began to grow louder; he was almost back. The last message was received at 4:58 p.m., August 30. *The day of the party.*

Camilla
Told Rupi about us (w/out mentioning ur name, like u asked). Let's just say she didn't react well.

My hands became increasingly shaky.
No. No. No.

In the footage from Esteban, it had been *Asher* who Camilla was talking about, not Mr. Bates. That must've been why he'd seemed so uncomfortable talking about

236

Camilla's confession, why he'd gotten up to "use the bathroom" when Rupi started discussing it. Asher could have planted the diary in Eric's room and told us it was Eric's handwriting. I bit down on my lip so hard that the metallic taste of blood lay on my tongue.

No. No. No.

My jaw agape, the phone fell from my hands, landing on its front screen.

"Bexley?" Asher hurried back in through the doorway and picked his phone up off the ground. "Shit, the screen is shattered. What the hell? Why are my old texts with Camilla open?"

I sat on the edge of his bed, unable to make eye contact with him. Mucus dribbled from my nose, salty tears saturating my face.

"Bexley?" He grabbed my shoulders. "Answer me."

I couldn't muster up words. All of me was shaking.

"Answer me! What happened?" When I finally shot a glance at his eyes, they were desperate. "What did you do?"

"What did *I* do?" I shook from his grip. "You're a liar. Are you a murderer, too?"

"What are you talking about?" He had to know what I was referring to; his texts with her remained open. "Okay, look, Bex, Camilla and I were a one-time thing. She lied all the time, even told me she and Rupi were already broken up, then switched her story a day later. I told you, she was always so dicey and secretive. I never meant to be a homewrecker." His words were fast, as if he had something to hide. Because he did.

It all made sense now—why he was so interested in

the case. He wanted to stray us from finding the true culprit: him. Did Venus know about Asher and Camilla? Was that why she'd acted so weird that day when I'd asked?

"How do you explain the orange note, then, huh?"

"The *what?*" Asher stood, looking handsome in his prince outfit while simultaneously looking like a coward. "What orange note?"

"The ink in Brandt's note was orange. I should've realized sooner. I can't believe I've been so stupid. I've let you betray, deceive, I—"

"Bexley, what are you talking about?"

"Stop playing dumb, Asher." The winged eyeliner and lengthening mascara I'd spent so long perfecting streamed down my face in thick, messy chunks. "I can't believe you."

"Bexley, please, can we talk about this? I—"

"There's nothing for you to say." I observed my haggard self in his full-length mirror, my makeup a mess, the artificial curls in my hair hanging stupidly around my face. Asher slid a hand around my waist, but I slapped it away.

"Ouch, Bex. Please—"

I rushed out of his room, lifting the bottom of my dress off the ground to prevent myself from tripping.

"Bexley!" he called, running after me. "Wait!" But his voice seemed cold. Maybe he'd been right when he'd said he didn't cry. Maybe he was cold at heart, and all the warmth he'd shown me had been fake.

I slipped out of the back entrance so none of his friends would ask any questions, Asher a few steps behind.

I need to find Brandt.

My feet going faster than my mind ever possibly could, I ran. Ran, ran, ran, until Asher couldn't find me. Until my breath quickened. Until my legs turned numb. Until I couldn't hear him anymore.

Asher is dead to me.

XVIII

The path is smooth that leadeth on to danger.
—Shakespeare, *Venus and Adonis*

T HE SUN STEADILY lowered in the sky, not quite set.

I needed to find the party, to warn Brandt that the note was from Asher. Though it was possible someone else had written the orange letter, Asher's other lies led me to easily believe that he would hide something like this, too.

Mr. Bates, now Asher, too? All while Camilla had been dating Rupi? Did people know this? Did the police?

Though there was no mirror anywhere, I could tell I looked horrible. Clenching my phone tight in my hand, my legs felt wobbly as I ran and ran across the dark campus, unsure of the location of the party—I should've checked out those flyers when I'd had the chance.

Just when I thought of collapsing and giving up, pounding music entered earshot. A vibration pulsed to my left, pulling me in that direction. I knew Brandt would be at the party, along with most of the seniors—the seniors who were stupid enough to attend a party after what had happened at the last one. Alerting Brandt of Asher's guiltiness was urgent; even though Asher was planning to stay in his room the whole night, he could have been working with others . . . others who would be at the party, awaiting Brandt's arrival.

What in the world could Asher's motive be?

But that didn't matter. Maybe he'd killed Eric out of love for Camilla, and Brandt somehow knew. Though the note implied he'd killed Camilla, too. All of that could be discovered later. Right now, I needed to save Brandt Harding before it was too late, just as I could've saved Abigail—*should've* saved Abigail. I still remembered the way the waves reflected the moonlight, that sour smell of the lake last fall.

The music became louder as I neared the boys' residence—another group's house that looked like Asher's, with white pillars and an ornate facade. The front door was wide-open.

I steeled myself and hurried into the party, greeted by blinding strobe lights, scattered red cups, and sweaty dancing bodies—just like August 30. I wondered whether this party was allowed. Where were the teachers? Glowing jack-o'-lanterns sat on counters, and fake spiderwebs draped beneath the ceiling.

Wait, are *they fake?*

Nobody noticed my entrance, and I was glad. Here, I was just another student, nothing strange or special about me. I jostled through the crowd, couples making out in every corner.

"Bexley."

Turning to the voice, I asked, "Who said my name?"

Brandt raised his hand, holding a red cup. "For you," he said as I stumbled toward him.

I took the cup from his hand and released it onto a tabletop with trembling hands, sending the liquid pouring out. "Oops. Listen, Brandt, I figured it all out," I said frantically.

"Figured what out?" He wore blue jeans and a football jersey: a lazy costume. "I think the two of us need to talk."

"I think so, too." I wanted to shout it out: *Asher did it! The note was from him!* But it wouldn't be advisable to let the whole senior student body know.

"Upstairs?" He cocked his head toward the stairway.

I nodded. Telling him was urgent.

Brandt led me into a dark and quiet room, the music faintly strumming through the walls. He flicked on the lights, but the room remained dim. I looked down at the stains of dust from snacks and spilled liquor that lined the hem of my gown. I collapsed, fatigued from running, onto the bed in the center.

He quickly locked the door behind him, the sharp metal clangs setting off warning signs within me. I hardly knew this kid. Still, I needed to get the truth out.

"Two words, Brandt—*Asher McCoy*," I said. "It all makes sense now. The note was orange, right? Who uses an orange pen? Right? His dad's company has an orange logo, and Asher gets orange merch all the time, including pens. And then this one time, I found this weird Shakespeare quote saying he was a devil pretending to be innocent or something weird like that in fancy language. And . . . And when your sister was dating Rupi, he was secretly with her. All of that added up . . . It has to be him."

"That was more than two words," he said, his stare unsettling as he moved toward the bed.

I didn't laugh.

"Okay, but really? Asher McCoy?" Brandt slapped his hand to his mouth, but the motion didn't seem genuine.

"I mean, what do *you* think?" I asked.

"I think . . ." He gazed out the window into the night. "I think you're right. It has to be him." He sounded like an inexperienced actor reading lines from a script.

"You don't sound convinced." The room was silent for a moment. "Well, we should at least leave this party before it's too late," I managed.

Still, Brandt stood stiff as a mannequin. As he turned to face me, I noticed the redness that brewed at the bottoms of his eyes.

"What's wrong?" A beat, and then, "There's something you're not telling me, isn't there?"

"No, no. I just . . . never thought Asher McCoy would have the heart to do it."

"Cut the shit," I said, surprising myself with the fierce language. I needed answers, and Brandt's eyes said he had them. "Tell me what you know."

A single tear trickled down his stubbled cheek. It seemed like forever before he spoke. "I didn't . . . I didn't mean to do it. It was an accident."

"Wait, what?" I stood, slowly walking backward, away from Brandt. "What didn't you mean to do?"

"It was just a fistfight. He was there in the bathroom, and I couldn't just . . ."

"Just what? Brandt, just *what*?" I yelled shrilly.

He was quiet for a moment as he started closing the distance between us, then wrenched my phone from my hand.

"What the hell are you doing?" I reached out, but he shoved the phone in his pants pocket. "Give it back."

"I need this to be just between us." His eyes were menacing.

The tip of an object glinted from his other pocket, but it was gone before I could consider anything. "Fine. Just tell me."

Is he getting at what I think he is?

"It wasn't during the fire drill. Earlier that day, I think. I was in the building talking to a teacher, and I went to the men's room, and . . . Some poor freshman found him in the bathroom after the drill." He paused.

"You can't just keep stopping right before you're about to actually say something." By now, my back was glued to the locked door. "Tell me what happened."

"Eric was there. It was just a fistfight at first." He flicked his eyes to a dusty corner of the room. "I knew it was him since the memorial assembly. He wouldn't look at me, and when I finally practically forced him to, his face turned tomato red. I'm not a man that goes purely off suspicion, so I did some digging. I found his ceramics knife in his backpack while he was in PE. It matched the way Cam got stabbed. The police showed me the reports, the files, pictures of the wound that made me fucking sick. It all matched up. But I couldn't tell them what I knew—not yet. Had to be sure first." He paused.

So you could be the hero.

I held my breath, hoping he'd continue. My heart thumped so loudly I could hardly think straight. The scary fact that I could be talking to a murderer dawned on me.

"He wouldn't look at me as he washed his fucking bloodstained hands," he continued, disgust in his tone. "I think he could feel my eyes on him, watching like a hawk. I threw the first punch." His eyes welled with more unshed tears. "When we were fighting, something went off in me. Like a light switch. A life in prison wasn't enough. No. He needed done what he did to Cam. He needed to pay. I don't think I even admitted that to myself as I was doing it. To outsiders, the beginning was like a playful brawl."

"And then you killed him, and you left him there," I finished, my breathing ragged. "You murdered Eric Fernsby. You—"

Brandt swiftly took a blade from his pocket, forcing a gasp out of me. "Shut your fucking mouth," he whispered, his voice low yet vehement. He didn't have to verbally threaten me; the knife spoke for him. Loudly.

Asher is innocent.

I bit down on my bottom lip so hard it began to bleed. "What's wrong with you?"

"Nothing. I—Something came over me. I couldn't stop punching and punching until the floor was all bloody and he wasn't breathing and . . . You have to understand, I hadn't intended to kill him." He stepped closer to me, an arm's length away now. "Cam had told me everything. Like how she and Eric had an unexpected friendship. She never told anyone because of Eric's asshole reputation. She thought their relationship was better off a secret. And then she drifted from him, when golf season was over.

But he'd opened up to her. Told her everything about his parents, how he had to live up to their impossible expectations or whatever. Boo-fucking-hoo. As time went on, he started hating Cam more and more. Jealous of her. Wanted her elite spot. He was crazy."

I swallowed. If he'd lost his temper once, he could do it again. I could be his next victim. "Was . . . Was that note fake?"

"I dug around, found out you were scrupulous." He cleared his throat, trying to look strong despite the tears and redness. "Along with other things. Other secrets. Asher made it so easy for me, leaving his pens sticking out of the pockets in his book bag. The feigned note succeeded in its mission—get you to attend this party and not have you suspect me."

"What? Why? Wait, you took his pens right out of his backpack—"

"What do you mean, why? You're the only person in the Academy so passionate about uncovering the case. You were so close to finding me. I didn't want to go to fucking prison."

"You won't get away with this." I tried to sound firm, but my shaky voice betrayed me. "What, you're gonna kill me, too? Someone else will find you. Asher knows I came here to talk to you. Venus will look for you. You can't just—"

"You think I wanna kill someone else? I'm not gonna murder you, Bexley."

A small bit of relief took the form of an exhale. "Why would you tell me, then?"

"I just said—you were so damn close to finding me.

What was next? You would've found something that led you to discover me as Eric's killer."

Knowing he wouldn't kill me at least gave me the confidence to say, "I'm telling the cops."

His eyes turned to slits as he approached me with the blade. "No, you're not." Brandt held the knife to my throat, so close that if I swallowed it might meet my skin. His breath was hot on my face. "You won't because I don't think you'd want them to know the truth about Abigail Delaney."

My heart dropped out of my chest. "You know nothing about Abigail."

He managed a sinister smirk, almost as if he were beginning to have fun with this. "I know more than you think."

So many things begged to escape my mouth—confessions, vulgar terms, cries for help—but all I managed was, "How?"

"An old friend of mine, Craig, is a cop. A couple months back, maybe even a year ago, we were hanging out, and he shoplifted some booze. Was always doing dumb shit. He was caught, but it could've cost him his job on the force, so I took the fall. Covered his ass. So when I asked him to do some digging, it was the least he could do. He didn't ask questions." Brandt paused. "It's nice to have people owe you favors. Just like Craig did. Just like you do now."

"I owe you nothing."

Ignoring me, he continued, "Not even he was able to find out the full truth. The full story about what happened to her."

"Nobody can."

"I don't think that's true." Brandt glared at me. "I think you know."

"No, I—" *have been lying to myself since it happened.* "I never found out."

"What did you do that night in your lake house, Bexley?"

"How do you—How do you know about this?" I stammered.

"Something was up with you. New senior at Grant Academy, and your best friend died last year? You were a mystery that I needed to solve. You slept at the Weinsteins' house, said you had no idea about the missing boat. She had alcohol in her system. The Weinsteins gave you an alibi, and you were off the hook."

A lone icy tear froze against my cheek. After we got out of the boat, I had run to the Weinsteins for help, and Abigail had run back to my house; we'd agreed. But the Weinsteins were best friends with my parents. I'd planned on telling them the truth, but as I approached—as they greeted me with warmth—I knew I'd already gotten away with it. I told them there was some creepy boat thief around, and they said they knew and insisted that I sleep in their guest room. They hadn't questioned me about the water on my shirt or my friend staying over. The memory made my heartbeat rapid. I'd ignored the real story for too long. When I'd told the police my false alibi, I'd almost convinced myself.

"There's no evidence. You can't prove anything," I said. The truth was out in the open for the first time, floating over me like a dark cloud. "It doesn't even matter anymore," I mumbled.

"Of course it does," said Brandt. "You're not such a saint, are you? You told the police that you left Abigail sleeping at your house and ran over to the Weinsteins. I don't buy it."

"Real alibi or not, she would've died either way," I blurted, surprising myself.

"So, you did? You're admitting that you lied to the police?"

"Maybe I did. Still, I don't know how she died. The last time I saw her, she was alive, running back for her phone. My mistakes don't even compare to what you did to Eric," I said. "I just—I kept myself safe. She would've wanted me to."

"Don't compare? I killed Eric for vengeance. You lied about Abigail for selfish reasons."

"You think I don't regret leaving her alone on the dock every single day? No. Don't twist this. Don't make me think I'm the bad guy here. You actively murdered Eric. Abigail . . . Abigail would've died either way. That doesn't matter. What you did, I can somehow prove. You can't prove anything about Abigail." I touched the scar on my knuckle, vignettes of the night coming to me in waves.

At once, Brandt pulled his phone from his jacket pocket and pressed a button, producing a beep. "Now I can. Nobody can refute a voice memo."

My hands clenched into fists. "Delete it."

"No way."

I lunged at him. "Don't show it to anyone. I'm begging you, please."

"I've got no problem with doing just that."

"As long as I don't tell the cops you killed Eric," I assumed.

"You're catching on."

"Screw you." I thought back to today's history lesson. That class seemed like ages ago now.

Mutually assured destruction.

"You won't tell them. Unless you want to go down with me," said Brandt, pocketing the knife; he didn't need it when his words were far more threatening.

I could put the past behind me, forget about Brandt and Camilla and Eric. It would be so easy, besides haunting me for the rest of my life. Or I could do what I knew was right.

I guess I'm going down with you, then.

I unlocked the door, Brandt muttering curses behind me.

XIX

Better three hours too soon than a minute too late.
—Shakespeare, *The Merry Wives of Windsor*

ONCE OUT OF the small room and in the bustling crowd downstairs, Brandt lost his power. I raced down the steps in the front of the house, Brandt barely behind me. It seemed like the run from Asher's to the party wouldn't be my only sprint of the night.

I worried that, once out in the black sky, I wouldn't be safe from Brandt. Still, I needed to get out of there. When I peered over my shoulder, I realized I wouldn't have that problem; Brandt had brought his car.

I have to get to the cops before he does.

It took him time to turn on his car, so I was a bit ahead of him, but that all changed once he began to drive. I ran as if it were life and death. It almost was.

I wasn't sure where the police would be, so I headed for the place I knew: Tuffin's office. She would be able to point me in the right direction.

The blue rock that lined the path rattled beneath my feet. I wanted to cry, to weep, but there was no time. Asher was perfectly innocent, and I'd acted so awful toward him. I shouldn't have been suspicious of Venus. Mascara streaked down my face again; I could feel it descending my cheeks. Saliva gathered by my chin.

The brass bell on the top of Linden Building came into view, providing a small bit of comfort. Brandt was nowhere to be found. Perhaps he knew where the detectives were and had gone straight to them.

I panted the whole way into Tuffin's office. There was no time to catch my breath. By a stroke of luck, she was still in her office at eleven o'clock.

I knocked violently on the door until she let me in, her brows furrowed. "Bexley, hello. That's a nice dress. What is it, dear? What's wrong? You look troubled."

"Yes." I nodded. "Where are the police? Where's Morales?" I said between breaths.

"Oh, Morales is staying in one of the cottages. I'm not sure about her assistant. Why don't you tell me what's wrong? Or would you like me to put you in touch with a guidance counselor instead?"

"Would you, by any chance, let me know which cottage?" I looked pleadingly at her.

"That would be a no. I'm sorry. I can summon her here if you'd like," Tuffin said kindly, her dark hair pulled into a bun. That wouldn't work. There was no time.

"Okay. Thank you, Headmistress Tuffin." My chest rapidly rose and fell. "I'll explain everything very soon. You're an amazing headmistress." All the cottages were in the same area; I could figure out which one was hers once I got there.

"Wait, Bexley—"

I raced to the cottages, letting the cool air whip my face. Mud drenched the bottom of the yellow dress at this point, but that was the least of my worries. The moment Brandt was arrested would be the moment I could breathe again.

As I ran through the night, some looked at me strangely, though nobody asked questions. As I turned the way to the houses, a shiny black car veered in the same direction. Beside the line of cottages, the vehicle slewed, and the tires skidded to a halt. Out came Brandt Harding. I was amazed I'd arrived at the same time as him; he must have made a wrong turn somewhere along the way or asked someone farther away for directions. That didn't matter now. What mattered was that I had a chance to get to Morales before him.

We locked eyes for a moment before I called, "Morales!" hoping she would hear.

Within moments, she creaked open her door. Her raven hair was tied in a bun atop her head, and a blue nightgown hung loosely on her body.

I ran toward her, breathing heavily. "Detective, I have to tell you something."

"Me, too," Brandt shouted. Clear liquid dribbled down his face; I couldn't tell if it was sweat, tears, or both.

Morales yawned, arching her brows in annoyance. "Fine. Come in. This better be good. How did you find out where I—"

"This is urgent," I said, pushing my way in front of Brandt.

Brandt offered me a lethal glare, as if he wished he'd killed me with the knife when he'd had the chance.

Morales's room was like a suite, grander than the already nice rooms of the students. She led us to a circular table and sat us down on chairs with paisley cushions. The aura of chamomile tea filled the air.

"Are you two just gonna sit there? Or do you have something to tell me?"

I locked eyes with Brandt. He mouthed something—I think it was "*We don't have to do this.*" I flicked my gaze away before I could change my mind.

"Two things, actually." I cleared my throat.

Am I actually doing this? Am I actually going to admit to a detective something I hardly ever admitted to myself?

"Brandt murdered Eric Fernsby. He beat him to death." I couldn't look at him; a tiny part of me pitied him. He'd been avenging his sister. Maybe there wasn't such a blatant binary of right or wrong. Maybe Brandt fell somewhere in between. Still, I couldn't take it back, and I didn't think I wanted to.

"You're really gonna do that? Fine, then Bexley—" Brandt paused, then resumed, "Bexley is at fault for—"

"I lied about what actually happened with Abigail Delaney," I said before he could. "Lock me up. I can't live with all this guilt inside me anymore." I dropped my head in relief. The truth was finally out, but dread filled me when I thought of my future.

Brandt slammed his fists on the table so loudly it probably woke the whole school. Now that we were in the company of Morales, though, his action bore little effect on me. He couldn't hurt me now.

"Oh my goodness." Morales's eyes widened. She kept her eyes on us while scouring the room for some handcuffs. After restraining our hands, she said, "I'm calling my assistant, putting on my uniform, then taking both of you off campus." She shook her head in utter disbelief. "Say your last goodbyes to the Academy, and don't expect to come back."

October 17, 1:34 a.m.

Last Year

"WHAT DO WE do, what do we do, what do we do?" Bexley asked, hoping her friend somehow had an answer. What would the police do to them?

"I don't know. Shit. Okay, um, let's turn, I guess." Even Abigail's voice sounded nervous. And she was never nervous. "Let's see how fast this son of a bitch can go."

Bexley plugged her ears and watched Abigail motor toward the dock. Pain pulsed through Bexley's right hand. They were going the same direction as the wind now, which helped them power to their destination.

"We'll be okay. Don't cry," Abigail said. It wasn't until then that Bexley realized the tears that soaked her cheeks. Were they due to the pain in her knuckle or the whole situation? Abigail and Bexley didn't need to do something "daring" to feel good about themselves. Why couldn't they have just relaxed in the lake house? Why couldn't that have been enough?

The police were gaining speed on them, so close Bexley and Abigail could feel their presence without turning to look. "Hey!" They heard the police from a distance away.

"Okay, listen, Bex. Your parents are friends with the Weinsteins, right? You're gonna run into their house and apologize and tell them to let you off the hook. I'm just the strange friend. I can't be there, okay? I'll run back into your lake house."

Bexley hesitated. "You're sure that's the best way?" she managed through tears.

"I'm not fucking sure, but we don't exactly have time to figure that out right now!" Abigail snapped. "Let's just—Let's get through this. It'll be fine, okay? Christ, stop crying."

Bexley nodded fiercely, wiping away her tears.

They slowed into the dock, not bothering to secure the boat with rope. There was no time for that. Abigail got out first, Bexley a few steps behind.

"Shit." Abigail suddenly pivoted and took her head in her shaking hands. "You go. I forgot my phone."

Bexley glared back at the boat. The flashlight from Abigail's phone sat upturned, waiting.

"Okay. Text me when you get back into the house."

Abigail watched Bexley escape toward safety. Her sweatshirt wasn't completely wet, but it was splashed by the waves in a few spots. Ditching her flip-flops, Abigail sprinted for her phone. The police were so close to the dock, and she wondered if they could make out her silhouette in the darkness that engulfed the night.

"Shit," Abigail repeated to herself, whispering as the police neared her. She wouldn't have time to get back to Bexley's house. That much was clear now. She also couldn't get Bexley in trouble for her own stupid idea.

Taking a long breath, Abigail silently thanked her parents for recently buying her a waterproof phone case. She braced herself for the cold and submerged beneath the water, save for just enough of her head so she could breathe. If she was hiding behind the boat, the police wouldn't be able to see her.

There were two of them, and as they approached, Abigail could hardly believe her ears. They were laughing. "They're just reckless—teens, probably," one said.

"Agreed," added the other, whose voice was a bit deeper. "Boat's back at the dock. Everything's returned. I say we leave it as is."

Abigail waited for the police to vacate the docks. They seemed to be taking their sweet time. Eventually, she swam toward and grounded her hands on the dock and tried to pull herself up. Intoxication still clouded her vision, veiling everything in front of her, but she'd make it. She kept telling herself that. It would all be okay once she was cuddled up in front of the fireplace, her bathing suit and sweatshirt on a drying rack.

"No. No, no, no, no, no." Her foot was stuck under the dock, lodged in between wood and metal and whatever it was that made docks. She kicked forward and backward, but her foot wouldn't budge.

She would text Bexley. Bexley could come out here and help her. The Weinsteins would, too. Just as the thought came, a wave came over, and the phone slipped right from her hands. Then came another one, strong enough to carry her phone an unfathomable distance away, strong enough to remove her foot from the dock, and strong enough to push her toward the boat. Her head knocked against the hard surface, and, after a great deal of pain, Abigail fell unconscious.

Bexley never got a text from Abigail. It wasn't until noon that she got a call, but that one was from the police, saying the words that would forever taunt her: "Abigail Delaney's body was found in the lake." But the unspoken part was the worst: *And it's your fault.*

XX

Three Days after Halloween

A LOT OF people said that the truth would set you free. Right now, I felt anything but free. Asher and Venus pretended to be understanding, yet I could see the disapproval, the disappointment that lurked behind their eyes. I couldn't blame them.

I thought about Abigail—words we'd shared, memories we had. If only we'd stayed inside that night, none of this would've happened. I'd still be at Vista High. This was my fault. "There's a lot I probably should've told you a long time ago." I could hardly make eye contact with Asher, which pained me.

Right now, Brandt was arrested, locked up, away. I kept wondering what would've happened if I'd remained quiet about him. Maybe things could've been different. I could still be studying at Grant Academy, my biggest problem a tedious English paper. But I couldn't. The guilt would weigh me down.

Asher and I stood by a marble fountain outside the Academy, November air cold against my face, rain falling down on us. He pulled me into a tight embrace. "This doesn't change how I feel about you," he whispered. "We can still see each other." But both of us knew it would never be the same.

"I was so quick to accuse you. I'm so sorry." I released my arms from around Asher and stepped back to look at him.

"You were under a lot of stress." He stared down at his hands. Forgiveness took time, and I was okay with that. "It hurt, but there were things I should've told you, too. Cami and I, for starters. I don't know why I held it in. There were a lot of times I wanted to tell you, but the words wouldn't come out."

Asher hadn't wanted to solve the case to hide his guilt-iness; he'd wanted to because he loved Camilla. Thinking about it shouldn't have stung as much as it did. We'd both made mistakes. Now it was time for me to pay. "You're pretty cool, you know."

He smirked. "I get that a lot."

I gave him a light punch in the chest before turning to find Venus approaching us. She wore her curls in a pony-tail and was clad in a neon pink sweatsuit. "So this is it?" As she came closer, I could see the redness that rimmed her eyes. "I'm not gonna have a roommate anymore?" Her usual cheery voice was laced with despair.

"Don't say that." I couldn't distinguish the rain from the tears that trickled down my face. "I'm sorry, really. I shouldn't have ever doubted you."

"It's okay. You did good, Bex. You're the most passion-ate person I know," said Venus. "You made a big change in just two months. And I'm glad that they finally took away the elite system." After the murders were solved, Grant Academy decided to do away with the selection of three elites; it was too competitive, too cutthroat.

"All right, Miss Windsor," Tuffin said, patting my back. I'd forgotten until then that she stood beside me.

"Wait!" It was Jessie, running over to us, along with Chase. They were both dressed in pajamas; it was barely breakfast time.

"I'm humiliated enough already. You don't need to do anything, Jessie," I managed, blinking back the tears that threatened to fall again.

"No, I . . ." She pursed her lips. "I was such a bitch to you. And I'm—I'm thankful. Thank you. Thank you for finishing this case when nobody else did."

Is this the same Jessie Rowley I know? And why do her words sound genuine?

"I . . . um . . . thanks?"

"Do you want to, like . . ." She awkwardly looped her arms around my back. After a second, she pulled back.

"I can't believe we just hugged," I mumbled.

"Me neither." She laughed. Not the sarcastic or sadis-tic laugh I'd grown accustomed to. This one was real, al-beit a bit sad.

"And I'm sorry I was an ass." It was Chase, taking me into a surprise hug.

"We all have our bad moments." I gave a half smile, patting his back.

"I should have trusted you." He took a slow step back. "You're making my boy happy, you're making me happy."

I nodded, not sure what was next for me. Where would I finish out my high school education after getting expelled from Grant? What college would take me now? Those were questions for another time, small compared to what had happened to Camilla, Eric, and Abigail. They would never get to go to college. A sense of numbness filled me.

"We're sorry to see you go, Miss Windsor," Tuffin said as if it had been my choice. "Your parents are parked in the lower lot." I took it as her signal that it was time to go.

"Okay," I responded, my voice breaking.

As we walked down, I kicked the blue rock and tried not to look back at my friends. It would be too painful. But in the end, I couldn't help sneaking one last glance. Venus, Jessie, and Chase were talking in a circle. Asher, though, stood separately, leaning against a tree. His eyes met mine, and I couldn't help noticing the tear that glided down his cheek.

So he did cry, after all.

ACKNOWLEDGEMENTS

Thank you so much for reading! I hope you enjoyed this story and that it kept you guessing. While this is my second published book, the process was in many ways different than that for *Not the Heir*. It involved a lot of time, editing, and people.

Without my beta readers, the story you just read would be a lot messier. Thank you so much to Lauren Redwood, Sophie Rinzler, Zoe Herman, Callie Duggan, MC Pending, Jill Adams, Laura Edwards, Meredith Tanowitz, Rachel Tanowitz, and Sasha Warm. Your early excitement helped me continue on this journey, and your honesty and critiques helped me craft this book into a better and cleaner novel.

Thank you, Lance Buckley, for creating the cover of my dreams. Thank you, Greg and Natalia at Enchanted Ink Publishing, for formatting *Academy for the Gifted* beautifully, proofreading with care, and helping me with the blurb. And thank you to Melissa McCoubrey, who diligently edited the manuscript. This book would not be a book without you guys!

To my family—thank you for the endless support. Mom, thank you for letting me ramble on about my ideas. Dad, thank you for helping me work through plot holes in the car. Sasha, thank you for reading this book in one day.

To my friends and family—even if you do not know it, you inspire me every day. Thank you for getting excited over Pinterest boards with me. For offering your opinions on the cover's early drafts. For interacting on my bookish Instagram. And finally, for just being there.

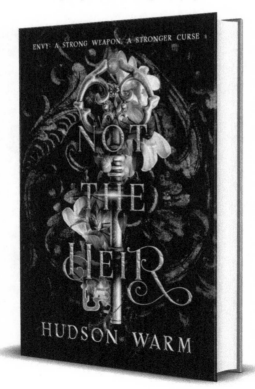

HUDSON WARM is a junior in high school in New York. Her debut young adult fantasy novel, *Not the Heir*, was awarded first place in the Purple Dragonfly awards for Youth Author Fiction and was featured on Katie Couric's "Books for Young Readers." Her poetry, flash fiction, and short stories have been recognized by the Scholastic Art & Writing Awards and have appeared in The Weight Journal, Cathartic Youth Literary Magazine, and other publications. Hudson won first prize for fiction in the 2021 Chappaqua Young Writer's Contest. She is also an editor for Polyphony Lit and The Vision. In addition to writing stories, Hudson enjoys writing and singing songs, which can be heard on most musical platforms. You can find her online at hudsonwarm.com or on Instagram @hudsonwarmbooks.

CPSIA information can be obtained
at www.ICGtesting.com
Printed in the USA
BVHW030255130122
626001BV00003B/242